D0090951

Also by Mark Griffiths

Space Lizards Stole My Brain!

Space Lizards Ate My Sister!

MARK GRIFFITHS

GEEK inc.

INVESTIGATING THE IMPOSSIBLE

TECHNOSLIME TERROR!

illustrated by Martin Chatterton

SIMON AND SCHUSTER

First published in Great Britain in 2013 by Simon and Schuster UK Ltd
A CBS COMPANY

1 3 5 7 9 10 8 6 4 2

Simon & Schuster UK Ltd
1st Floor, 222 Gray's Inn Road
London
WC1X 8HB

Simon & Schuster Australia, Sydney
Simon & Schuster India, New Delhi

A CIP catalogue record for this book
is available from the British Library.

PB ISBN: 978-0-85707-537-6
eBook ISBN: 978-0-85707-538-3

Printed and bound by CPI Group (UK) Ltd, Croydon, CR0 4YY

www.simonandschuster.co.uk
www.simonandschuster.com.au

For Laura

With thanks to Kate at the Viney Agency,

Jane and Kat at Simon & Schuster,

Martin Chatterton and Jo Beggs.

PROLOGUE

Lewis Grome awoke to find himself on fire.

He stared, bleary-eyed and blinking, at the bright yellow flame dancing along the leg of his shabby school trousers and wondered what, if anything, he should do about it.

It was a warm September evening and he was lying on his back in a wide grassy field bordered by neatly trimmed hedgerows. Above him, the sky was an unending expanse of blue interrupted only by a worrying ribbon of thick black smoke. The air was still and swallows skimmed the ground. A butterfly jittered past on wings the colour of scrambled egg.

The flame on Lewis's trousers crackled. Lewis tried to ignore it but he knew he was only putting off the inevitable. He reached out a cautious hand and patted his leg. The flame died away quickly. He withdrew his hand and looked at it. The centre of the palm was black with soot but there was no pain in either his hand or his leg. On the back of his hand was a strange blue mark about the size of a penny. It looked a little like a flower – a daisy perhaps? He held the hand up to his face to get a better look but as he did so, the blue mark seemed to shimmer and fade away. He frowned, examining both sides of his hand again. But the strange blue mark had vanished.

Clambering to his feet, Lewis picked up his schoolbag, which was now lying next to him, and checked inside. Sandwiches, *Chocky-Crocky* bar, can of drink, books, pencil case. All in order.

Lewis was eleven years old, short for his age, with a round, pudgy face and an untidy spray of fair hair. The school uniform he wore was ill-fitting and threadbare, a grubby patch of white shirt visible through the frayed elbow of his jumper.

He looked at the wreckage of the lorry, which lay sprawled before him on the grass like the decaying carcass of an enormous beast, and at the column of oily black smoke that puffed from the charred remains of its fuel tank, and suddenly remembered what had happened.

He had been walking in the lane near his house, sauntering home from school, when he heard the lorry approaching from behind. Lorries often used the lane as a shortcut from the town to the motorway, so he wasn't surprised to hear one coming. He stepped out of its path automatically, flattening himself against the hedgerow, waiting for it to pass. But the lorry never came. Instead, Lewis heard its brakes emit a sudden piercing shriek that sent a cold thrill surging through his entire body. He had turned just in time to see the lorry skidding into the hedgerow. It looked like the driver had swerved to avoid something in the road – some small dark object – and lost control of his vehicle. Lewis could only watch as the lorry smashed through the hedgerow into a field, its length first folding and then splitting into two sections – jackknifing, that was the term they always used on the news, he had thought – and then toppling over on to its side with a sound of tortured metal and shattering glass. The lorry had rolled several times before becoming still.

Sprinting towards the huge ragged hole the lorry had torn in the hedgerow, Lewis tried to get a closer look. His heart pounding, he stepped through into the field. As he did so, two things happened in quick succession. The first was that, from the corner of his eye, he saw the object that the driver had been so keen to avoid. It was a squirrel, and it was crouching in the centre of the narrow lane. Oblivious to the carnage it had caused, it regarded Lewis with glassy, unknowing eyes and then scurried away, its long soft tail rippling.

The second thing that happened was that the lorry's fuel tank chose that moment to explode.

Now, his head clearer, Lewis paced in a slow circle round the wreckage of the lorry, ignoring the smell of singed nylon rising from his trousers. The explosion had been a small one. A few patches of grass around the vehicle were still charred and smoking. In other places, strange patches of undamaged bare earth were visible, as if the grass covering them had simply vanished. The lorry itself was still mostly intact, save for the fact that its container section had snapped in two. The driver's cab lay on its side surrounded by the smashed remains of its windscreen, the shards of glass gleaming like chips of ice. Lewis peered inside. A large man in grey overalls sat in the driver's seat, his hands still clutching the steering wheel, as if the lorry's current predicament were no more than a tight parking space that he might manoeuvre out of with a little concentration. He was horribly still.

The container section of the lorry was made of thin metal and painted white. It had broken midway along its length. Lewis peeked inside both halves. Empty. He was about to turn and leave when he heard a noise: a slow, steady pattering. It was coming from the far end of the container's rear half. Curious, he climbed into the container, his school shoes clattering against the metal.

There in the corner lay a grey metal box about the size and shape of a safe. It was hidden in the semi-darkness, so he had missed it on his initial inspection. Odd, he thought, that this huge lorry had been used to transport this one fairly small object. There was a door set into the box's front, although it seemed to have no dial or keyhole or even any handle. The door had buckled in the crash and hung limply on one of its two chunky metal hinges. Within the box, Lewis could make out an unidentifiable blue shape. He swung open the damaged door. Inside was a squat cylindrical container made of sturdy transparent plastic. It was filled with a viscous blue liquid, which was slowly dripping out through a deep, jagged crack in the front, creating slow, circular ripples in a thick blue puddle beneath.

He rummaged in his schoolbag and pulled out the first thing that came to hand, one of his school textbooks. He tore out a page and allowed a single drop of the thick blue liquid to fall on to it.

CHAPTER ONE
THE GRANDFATHER CLOCK

The girl watched as the warm morning breeze whirled dust around the base of the grandfather clock. Blinking away the tears, she took a tissue from her bag and blew her nose. The clock's face read ten past eight. Plenty of time before school to linger.

The grandfather clock stood in the centre of a patch of wasteland near the edge of town; a square of bare, cracked concrete hidden from the road by trees and a tall fence, dotted with litter, weeds and broken bricks. The clock was tall, nearly two metres, and made of a rich, dark wood. Its long case was slender and well proportioned. Two elaborately wrought needle-like hands crossed its face. It was probably very old, thought the girl, or at least a copy of something very old.

But what was it doing here?

She closed her eyes in concentration, mentally filtering out the growl of distant traffic and the chatter of magpies in the nearby trees, until all she could hear was the deep, stately beat of the clock's ticking.

That was the other odd thing: it was ticking.

Here was a beautiful old grandfather clock standing in the middle of nowhere, quietly ticking away the minutes and hours to itself, offering no clue as to how it had got here or to whom it might once have belonged.

Despite her tears, the girl found herself laughing at the sheer peculiarity of it all. This was the third morning in a row she had come to this place and each time she had been surprised and delighted to find the clock still here. It was a thing out of place, an oddity.

She knew how that felt.

The girl breathed in deeply, letting the sound of the clock's gentle ticking fill her mind and body until it became like a second heartbeat.

For the past two mornings, the young man had been waiting for her outside her house in a car. He had long, greasy hair and a thin strip of fluff on his top lip that held ambitions to be a moustache. He was armed with a digital camera and kept trying to take her photograph as she walked to school. The girl had told him that she didn't want to be photographed; she wanted to be left alone so she could walk to school in peace. But the young man just laughed and asked her to smile, all the while continuing to take her photo. When she ran, he followed in his car. When she screamed at him to go away and stop harassing her, he laughed again and said he was just doing his job and that she shouldn't be such a freak if she didn't want to be treated like this. Each morning she had managed to lose him by slipping through a gap in the fence next to the railway bridge and then crossing the patch of wasteland. And each morning she had found the grandfather clock waiting patiently there for her. Seeing it was becoming a ritual, she realised, one that helped her to forget the unpleasant earlier encounters and prepare for the day ahead.

A sudden tuneful clang made the girl's eyes snap open. The clock was striking; it was a quarter past the hour. She hadn't heard it do that before. The chime was lovely, a dignified echo of some age long gone. She smiled, enjoying the miniature musical performance – and then frowned, shaking her head in puzzlement. She twiddled a strand of her hair thoughtfully.

Something wasn't right.

The girl got down on her knees and examined the base of the clock and the ground around it. Behind the clock were a few dandelions, each one a few metres apart from its neighbour, forming a rough straight line. She had noticed this row of yellow flowers yesterday. The clock was level with the third dandelion. She checked again. Definitely the third. There were no severed stalks in the line where a dandelion might have been growing recently until nibbled away by some passing creature, and she was pretty sure that dandelions couldn't sprout and bloom in a single day. She hadn't made a mistake. What she was observing was a fact. There was no other explanation. She gave a nervous laugh.

The clock had moved since yesterday.

CHAPTER TWO
HONOURABLE DEATHS

If there was anything fun about being in Year Eight at Blue Hills High School, Barney Watkins had yet to discover it. True, he had only been at the school less than a fortnight and hadn't been looking very hard, but nothing he had encountered during that time had given him cause for hope.

It was lunchtime and Barney was sitting alone in the playground with his back to the wall. He was of average height, button-eyed and snub-nosed in a way that endeared him to older sisters, mothers and grandmothers. Despite the near deafening noise of the children playing around him, all his attention was focused on the screen of his mobile phone.

Blue Hills High was a collection of grime-smeared sandstone buildings surrounded by tall iron railings. It was a small school and all the children seemed to know each other. None, though, had shown any interest in getting to know Barney.

Not that he cared. He had plenty of friends already, ones he had grown up with at his old school in Kent. There was Michael Taylor, with whom he played badminton and acted in silly plays they wrote together; Richard Lee, a would-be businessman who spent his spare time hunting for lost golf tees on a nearby course and then selling them back to the players; and Darryn Lavery, who loved to fish in the local brook in search of sticklebacks. Three interesting, devoted mates who made him laugh and who stuck up for him in fights. There was just one tiny problem, though, and that was the fact that since Barney's family had moved to the small town of Blue Hills in north-west England three weeks ago, because of his father's new job, Michael, Richard and Darryn were now over 200 miles away.

Barney scrolled through the photographs stored on his phone: images of him and his friends messing about with a hosepipe and water pistols in his garden one summer afternoon. The photos had seemed forgettable at the time, but now they felt like sacred historical documents to Barney – a solemn reminder of a life he no longer had. Of course, he still kept in touch with his friends online, but it just wasn't the same as before.

Still, it was all he had.

A foot tapped Barney's elbow, pulling him from his thoughts.

'Put that away,' said a voice. 'No phones allowed in school. If Gloria sees that, you'll be for the high jump.'

Barney looked up and saw a tall, thin boy standing over him. He had closely cropped red hair and a freckly nose. The boy's expression was blank, not outwardly hostile but not friendly either.

'Sure,' said Barney, pocketing the phone. 'Thanks for the warning. What does this Gloria teach?'

The boy snorted. 'Come on. We're playing Honourable Deaths.'

'I don't really feel like playing anything, thanks.'

'Yeah, like you have a choice,' said the boy and hauled Barney to his feet by the collar.

The tall boy with the freckles, whose name it turned out was Duncan, marched Barney over to a group of older boys who were waiting in a corner of the playground. They grinned when they saw him.

'Go up there,' said Duncan and pushed Barney towards a wheelchair ramp leading to a fire exit at the back of the school canteen.

'I really don't want to play,' said Barney. 'Sorry. Nothing personal, guys.'

'We're just trying to be friendly to a new kid,' said Duncan with a sickly smile. 'Now go up there.'

Barney heaved a sigh and trotted up the ramp. 'What do I do?'

The boys cackled with laughter.

'You die,' said Duncan. 'Here,' he said, 'have a hand grenade,' and threw one at Barney.

Barney opened one eye, keeping the other squeezed tightly shut. Light streamed in, white, foggy and confused. He allowed the blurred image on his retina to resolve itself and saw the group of boys standing at the bottom of the ramp. They were falling about with laughter.

'Go on,' said Duncan. 'Die!'

Barney squinted at him. 'I'm sorry?' he said.

'Look, you little *moron*. I've just thrown a *hand grenade* at you. Now you have to *die*.'

Barney looked down at the ground, frowning. 'Have you?' he said.

'Not a real one, you berk!' said Duncan.

'Oh,' said Barney. 'I see.'

'The genius gets it,' said Duncan, turning to the other boys and clapping sarcastically. 'So now you have to die. Go on.'

'Right,' said Barney and staggered back against the fire exit, groaning.

The boys jeered. 'Pathetic,' said Duncan. 'Put a bit of effort into it. You've just been blown up by a hand grenade. Explode!'

Barney straightened up. 'Right, gotcha,' he said. 'How about this?' He threw himself into the air, arms wheeling, and made a loud, spittle-fuelled noise like an explosion.

Duncan shook his head. 'You look like my uncle dancing at a wedding,' he said. The other boys sniggered. 'But,' he went on, 'we haven't got all day, have we, genius? Make this one better. All right, next!' He stood aside and let another boy take his place opposite Barney at the bottom of the ramp.

This boy was squat and pug-like, with tight brown curly hair. 'Kalashnikov AK-47,' he barked and mimed shooting Barney with a machine gun, spraying him with imaginary bullets and making a high-pitched staccato noise.

Dutifully, Barney writhed and screamed as if being hit by a fusillade of machine-gun fire, before collapsing in a heap on the ramp.

'You haven't got a clue,' said the brown-haired boy. He spat on the ground and gave way to the next in line.

'Dagger to the throat,' said the next boy. Wearily, Barney got to his feet.

Lunchbreak wore on. The boys chopped off Barney's limbs with imaginary axes; they gutted him with imaginary broadswords; they watched with disdain as he died slowly and painfully from imaginary poison, kicking and convulsing.

'You're not very good, are you?' said Duncan when all the boys had taken a turn. 'I've never seen such bad dying.'

'Sorry,' muttered Barney, rubbing his elbow. He was sore all over from continually throwing himself on the ground. 'It's not something I've had much practice at.'

Duncan glanced at his watch. There were only a couple of minutes to go before the end of lunchbreak. 'OK,' he said. 'Last chance, genius. I'm going to chuck another hand grenade and this time I want you to blow up like you mean it. You got me?'

Barney nodded. Then his attention was distracted by a sudden flash of white light at the opposite end of the playground. Shielding his eyes from the sun, he squinted into the distance. It was a small white bird with a long, streaming white tail, unlike any bird Barney had ever seen before. He could just make out a smallish boy standing alone nearby watching the bird as it swooped and flitted. The boy clicked his fingers and the bird fluttered towards him obediently and then disappeared inside his schoolbag. The boy slung the bag over his shoulder and hurried towards the school building. It was then that Barney recognised him. They were in the same form.

'Did you see that?' Barney asked the other boys, pointing. 'Lewis Grome has got a trained bird in his schoolbag! A bird!'

'Put a sock in it!' barked Duncan. 'Now get ready!' He mimed plucking a hand grenade from a box of ammunition. He tossed and caught it a few times in one hand and then raised it to his mouth and pulled out the pin with his teeth. He drew back his arm and hurled the invisible grenade at Barney with all his force, covering his ears with his hands.

This time Barney was ready. In slow motion, he reacted to the oncoming grenade, a look of horror dawning across his face. He crouched into a protective ball, as he imagined a soldier might do in such a situation. Then, with an ominous rumbling that began in his belly and grew steadily in volume and intensity, the noise of the explosion began to erupt from inside him. As the sound swelled, so did his panic, his eyes growing huge, his mouth opening wide in a scream ... building ... building ... to a nerve-shredding crescendo of pure terror. And then the blast hit him. With shocking suddenness, he flung back his head, his arms. He was a sapling in the throes of a hurricane. He was a matchstick caught in a tornado. No one, Barney was making clear, had ever been blown up by a hand grenade quite as thoroughly and spectacularly as he himself was now being blown up. He railed and reeled, shaping the sound of the explosion with his mouth like a musician modulating the tone of his instrument, spraying out a fine mist of saliva droplets, and then hurled himself against the fire exit as hard as he could. He ricocheted off the door, the air slamming from his lungs, and fell on to the ramp with a painful crunch.

He lay there motionless for a moment, panting, to allow the magnitude of his performance to sink in.

When he looked up, the others had gone.

He stood up and brushed himself down, feeling his face redden. A light tinkling sound came from his coat pocket. Curious, he put his hand in and drew out the smashed remains of his mobile phone.

CHAPTER THREE
GABBY

When lunchtime came the next day, Barney loitered inside the main school building, hoping to stay out of the imaginary weapon sights of Duncan and his friends. He roamed the empty corridors, his footsteps echoing on the dusty floor, and felt like some lonely ghost condemned to wander around the building until the end of time – or at least until afternoon registration.

As he neared the front entrance, Barney

suddenly heard voices and saw a weary-looking member of staff with a ragged beard and a mug of coffee shooing pupils outside into the playground. Barney ducked round a corner and saw some more kids studying a notice outside the head teacher's office. He sidled up and stared at the piece of paper. If nothing else, he figured, standing here all lunchtime was preferable to going outside.

The notice was a list of lunchtime clubs pupils could join:

BLUE HILLS HIGH

LUNCHTIME CLUBS – AUTUMN TERM

CHESS CLUB – ROOM U15

SALSA DANCING – ROOM U05

CHOIR – SCHOOL HALL

PHOTOGRAPHY – ROOM U19

NETBALL – SPORTS HALL

ARTS & CRAFTS – ROOM U07

SCHOOL NEWSPAPER – ROOM LD1

DRAMA – ROOM L5

None of these activities held much interest for Barney, but he would gladly have spent every lunchtime for the rest of his schooldays learning salsa dancing in a room full of girls than play another game of Honourable Deaths. He scanned the list a few times, trying to decide which of the clubs would involve the least effort. *Drama maybe?* Then he noticed some writing at the very bottom of the notice. Someone had added in blue biro, in very neat, friendly handwriting, the words:

Geek Inc. Investigating the impossible! – Room U13.

And beneath that someone had scrawled in pencil:

Weirdo.

Barney blinked at it. *Geek Inc.?*

'Come along, you lot,' said the teacher with the ragged beard. 'You can't hang about in the corridor all day. Get yourselves off to a club or get yourselves outside.'

The group of children dispersed.

The door to room U13 was ajar. Barney peered round it and saw a girl sitting at a desk reading a magazine. Her pale skin had olive undertones. A tangle of thick brown curls reached past her shoulders. Perched on the bridge of her thin nose was a pair of small circular glasses that reminded Barney of one of the men on the cover of his mum's Beatles CDs. Barney guessed that she was at least a year older than him. The girl toyed absently with a strand of her hair.

Barney tapped at the door lightly with his fingertips.

The girl looked up. 'Yes?' She did not sound welcoming.

'Is this Geek Inc.?' He felt self-conscious saying the words out loud.

'Yes.'

'I'd like to join I think. I need to do something at lunchtimes.'

The girl fixed him with a look. 'Do you believe in ghosts, werewolves, vampires, flying saucers, ESP, time travel, reincarnation and the Loch Ness Monster?'

'Er, well' said Barney. 'Dunno.'

'Good,' said the girl. 'Then you're in.'

Barney blinked. 'Oh. Thanks!'

'The thing is,' said the girl, putting down her magazine, 'that most people have already made up their minds on those issues, even though they haven't looked at all the evidence. That's really stupid. And it's one reason why this planet is in the state it is. But clearly, you're an intelligent sort. You want to investigate, find out the truth for yourself. That's good. What's your name?'

'Barney,' said Barney. 'Barney Watkins.'

'Gabby Grayling,' said the girl, extending a hand. 'Pleased to meet you.'

Barney shook it. He had never shaken hands with a girl before. It was an oddly thrilling and grown-up experience.

'So – erm – what exactly is Geek Inc.?' The notice said something about you investigating the impossible?'

Gabby laughed. 'That's right. I'm into anything – absolutely *anything* – that defies explanation. Something that shocks, confuses and twists your brain. Something that, when you see it, makes you think the world is far weirder and more amazing than you thought it was when you woke up that morning. Imagine if a worm spoke to you. Or if the moon suddenly sneezed.' She grinned broadly. 'That would be impossible, wouldn't it?'

Barney nodded slowly. 'OK – and has anything impossible like that ever happened to you?'

Gabby grinned. 'Do you believe in levitation, Barney?'

'Umm, again I'm not a hundred per cent certain either way.'

'Excellent!' said Gabby. 'We don't just blindly believe impossible stuff at Geek Inc.. We *investigate* it. Check this out.' She got up out of her chair and stood in the corner of the room, flexing her arms.

'Who's "we"?' said Barney, looking around the empty room. 'Do you have many members?'

Gabby closed her eyes and started breathing deeply. 'At the moment there's just two of us. The President of the club – that's me – and our Vice-president.'

'Who's the Vice-president?'

'That would be you, Barney. Welcome aboard.'

'What?'

'Watch,' said Gabby. 'Watch and be astounded.'

'But—'

Gabby waved a hand to silence him. She took a deep breath and held out her arms like a tightrope walker. '*Watch*,' she whispered.

Barney watched. Nothing happened. *Uh-oh*, he thought. Now he knew why someone had written *weirdo* on the notice. Coming here had been a waste of time after all. Maybe the choir would let him join if he promised to just stand at the back and mime.

But then slowly, *very* slowly, Gabby's feet began to lift off the floor until she was floating about ten centimetres above it. Barney let out a whimper.

'No way!' he gasped. 'No *way*! You're doing it! Really doing it!' He steadied himself against a table. His legs felt like they were melting. '*No. Way!*'

Gabby bobbed up and down very gently. 'Do you believe in levitation now?' she asked. 'Do you believe the evidence of your own eyes, hmm?'

'Oh, wow, yes,' said Barney. 'Yes. Oh, wow. Oh ...' Speech was beginning to fail him. 'How do you ... *do* it?' he said finally.

She lowered herself to the ground in a swift, graceful movement. 'I don't,' she said. 'It's a cheap trick.'

'I don't understand,' said Barney, scrunching his forehead.

'It's called Balducci levitation. Look it up. It's no secret.'

'You mean you didn't actually levitate?'

'No,' said Gabby. 'I didn't.'

'Not even a little bit?'

She laughed. 'Not even a little bit. The point is, Barney, sometimes the evidence of our eyes can be deceptive. What we may think is truly weird or impossible may turn out to be something much more mundane.'

'So you don't believe in UFOs or any of that stuff, then?'

'I believe in UFOs, sure,' she said, grinning.

'You do?'

'Of course. UFO just means Unidentified Flying Object. Are there flying objects out there that have not been identified? Yes, lots. Do I believe they are alien spaceships? Well, that's another question. Show me the evidence that they are and I might. That's how we roll at Geek Inc..'

'You look for evidence of alien spaceships? Cool!'

Gabby chuckled. 'We look for evidence of anything odd or impossible. And remember, absence of evidence is not evidence of absence.'

'I see,' said Barney. He didn't at all, but he was having such a good time that he didn't want to spoil it. The first week of term at his new school had not yet ended and already he had been made Vice-president of a school club and shaken hands with a girl. Things were looking up. 'I do have another question though,'

'Sure, go ahead. All questions are welcomed here,' Gabby replied.

'Why is the club called Geek Inc.? I mean, it's not exactly "cool" is it?'

'It is to me, Barney. That's the whole point. Everyone in this school seems to thinks I'm a geek for not being obsessed with make-up or fashion or whatever the latest Z-list celebrity is up to. So I thought, why fight it? Why not use the name for a club that's all about stuff that's *really* cool – the bizarre, the impossible and the odd? So that's what I did. Yeah, I'm a geek – and proud of it, mate.'

Barney thought about this for a moment. Weirdly it seemed to make perfect sense. Suddenly he remembered the events in the playground a couple of days ago. 'Would you say a boy with a trained bird that obeys his commands comes under the heading "bizarre, impossible and odd"?' he asked.

'What?'

'There's a boy called Lewis Grome – some kids call him Grimy Grome . . .'

'I know who you mean,' said Gabby. 'The one always eating *Chocky-Crocky* bars. I've seen him. Small. Tatty uniform. Personal hygiene issues.'

'That's him. He keeps a little white bird in his schoolbag. I saw it yesterday. Fluttering about the playground. He snapped his fingers and it flew right into his bag.'

'That's crazy! Why does he bring a bird to school?'

Barney shrugged.

'You should investigate! Find out what's going on.'

Barney considered this. 'Maybe I will.'

The five-to-one bell rang to signal that lunchtime was nearly over.

'Time to go,' Barney said. 'When do we meet next?'

'Arranging the club's meeting schedule is the job of the Vice-president. You tell me.'

'I'll draw up a timetable,' said Barney, happy to have a simple, practical task to carry out. A thought occurred to him. 'How do I get in touch with you?'

'You got a mobile?'

Barney shook his head. 'It died.'

'In that case,' said Gabby, 'come here.' She fished a biro out of her bag and jotted some digits on the back of Barney's hand, the pen's metal tip cold and hard against his skin. 'There,' she said. 'Call me. Text me. Whatever.'

'I will,' said Barney, reading the number. Her handwriting was neat and friendly. 'Thanks for letting me join the club.'

'Thanks for being worth having in it.'

'See you later, then.'

'See you,' said Gabby. 'Oh. One more thing.'

'Yes?'

'Meet me at the school gate at home time this afternoon. There's something I want to show you.'

'Something impossible?'

'Pretty much.'

CHAPTER FOUR
GLORIA

In the general science lesson that afternoon, Barney's pencil rolled off the table he was sharing with Lewis and rattled on to the floor. Barney turned to Lewis and tutted, rolling his eyes as if to say *Cuh! What an idiot, eh?*, and sank below the table to retrieve it.

Crouching on his hands and knees on the dusty floor, Barney grinned and silently congratulated himself on his own cleverness. Lying next to his pencil under the table was the squashy red form of Lewis's schoolbag, its top lolling open like a mouth.

He had tried asking Lewis directly about the bird during afternoon registration, but Lewis wouldn't co-operate, answering his every question with weird, cryptic remarks about clouds and stars and giggling to himself in an odd, distracted way. Barney couldn't tell if Lewis was a bit crazy or was simply making fun of him. Determined to impress Gabby by uncovering the truth about the bird, he had devised this somewhat simple ploy to look inside Lewis's schoolbag.

Barney prised open the bag with slow, careful fingers and peered inside. A sudden thought struck him. What would he do if the bird started flapping and squawking here in the classroom? What if it bit him? He paused, holding his breath. Perhaps if the bird were trained to stay quiet in the bag all day, it wouldn't mind being disturbed now? He sorted gingerly through the bag's contents, half expecting a sharp beak to nip at his fingers at any moment. *Can, Chocky-Crocky bar, some books, a sheet of crumpled paper* That was it. That was all that was inside. Had Lewis not brought his bird to school today?

Lewis let out a shrill giggle. Barney's heart thumped and he clambered to his feet hurriedly, conspicuously brandishing his pencil, and sat down. A few of the other kids were glancing over at Lewis with amusement – and then shooting nervous glances at the tiny girl sitting near the back of the classroom. The girl looked up and narrowed her eyes. Everyone returned their gaze to their books.

Barney frowned. He did not know the girl's name. She was in a different form to him and so he only saw her in certain lessons where pupils from several different forms were combined into a single large class. She had straight blonde hair and wore an Alice band. Her features were regular and pleasing, her eyes big and blue. In fact, thought Barney, she seemed quite sweet in an old-fashioned *Famous Five* sort of way. But her presence always had a strangely unnerving effect on those around her. Smiles evaporated. Gazes dropped. Jokes petered out.

Their science teacher, Mr Osborn, had left the room for a few minutes. In most lessons this would have been a cue for anarchy to break out, but Barney was surprised to find work continued as normal in his absence, with the class working as conscientiously as if they were sitting an exam.

All except Lewis, that was. He was playing with a small metal pencil sharpener, pushing it around the table as if it were a car racing round a track, making engine noises and giggling to himself. The pencil sharpener had two dots of correcting fluid dabbed on it that represented headlights, or possibly even eyes.

Lewis tapped Barney's arm. 'It's tired,' he

whispered. 'So I have to move it myself. Shame it hasn't got a sail like a boat. I could blow on it.' At this he burst into a loud guffaw that echoed round the classroom. Muted gasps of astonishment came from some of the other children. Lewis clapped a hand to his mouth, but all this did was turn his guffaw into a series of hoarse, wet sniggers.

A chair scraped against the floor. The sound set Barney's teeth on edge. He turned round to see the tiny blonde girl walking up to their table. Lewis paid her no attention and continued pushing around the pencil sharpener, still smirking.

'Put that away and get on with your work, Lewis,' the girl said very quietly. Her voice was low and brimming with confident authority. Lewis ignored her. '*Now*, please, Lewis . . .' she added, her tone firmer.

Lewis looked up. 'Float away, man,' he said in a

dreamy voice. 'You're really very small.' This prompted another gasp from the class.

The girl fixed him with her big blue eyes. 'Put that away now and get on with your work, Lewis,' she said, speaking very slowly and deliberately, 'or you will regret it.'

'Come on now,' Barney heard himself say in a cheery voice. 'Leave Lewis alone. He's not harming anyone, is he?' He felt absurd talking to this tiny girl as if she were some terrifying thug who might lash out at any moment. He smiled at her weakly and then looked down at his school tie. The upside-down image of a swooping eagle on the Blue Hills High School crest stared back at him, mocking him with its effortless ferocity.

The tiny girl turned her big blue eyes on Barney. 'We haven't met,' she said. 'My name's Gloria. I edit the school newspaper, the *Blue Hills High Examiner*.' She held out her hand.

'Barney,' he said, shaking her hand. *Twice in one*

day, he thought. Then he realised he had heard her name somewhere before.

'If people break the school rules, it all goes in the *Examiner*, Barney,' said Gloria. 'It's my job to report it. Every last embarrassing little thing. People have a right to know, don't you think, what goes on in their own school? What kind of person they might be sitting next to in a lesson?'

Barney shrugged.

'Our readers love it,' continued Gloria. 'The more disgraceful the revelations about their classmates, the more they lap it up and the more the *Examiner*'s circulation increases. If I want, I can utterly humiliate anyone I choose simply by telling the right unhappy truth about them. And believe me, I will find out what that is. Did they wet themselves once in junior school? Did they once call a teacher "Mummy"? Have they ever stolen so much as a single crayon from an art supplies cupboard? Any deviation from the path of decency can be thrown back at someone a thousand-fold simply by reporting it. It does wonders for school discipline. So please bear that in mind next time you start sticking your adorable little nose in my business, Mr Barney Watkins, ex-pupil of Greenleaf Primary in Kent.'

Barney gasped. 'How do you know so much about me?'

Gloria smiled. 'A good reporter never reveals her sources.' Then, in a deft movement, she snatched the pencil sharpener out of Lewis's hand and tossed it with a clang into the large metal bin at the side of Mr Osborn's desk.

Barney looked at his watch. It was nearly fifteen minutes since the final bell of the school day had sounded. The torrent of children streaming out through the gate had slowed to a trickle of dawdlers and those kept behind after class.

He watched as a group of sixth-formers

sauntered from their own building towards the scrubby patch of grass where their cars were parked. One of them seemed much shorter than all the others. It was Gloria, Barney realised. It looked as if she was remonstrating with the older pupils, waving her arms about and shouting, clearly upset about something, but about what Barney couldn't tell. The sixth-formers looked down at the ground, shuffling their feet and not meeting her eye. With astonishment, Barney realised she was telling them off.

From out of nowhere a white shape, sleek and fast as a dart, hurtled through the air and connected with the back of Gloria's head. Barney recognised it instantly. Gloria yelped and clawed at her hair. The sixth-formers tried to help, but she waved them away. Again the white bird flashed, swooping and buzzing at Gloria, nipping at her head and arms. The others reached for the bird, but it darted upwards, tiny wings fluttering madly.

Gloria sprang into the air and swiped a hand at the bird. She missed it by millimetres, landing back on the ground with a frustrated grunt. The bird hovered overhead for a moment, as if taunting her, and then streaked off into the distance and vanished through the railings. His eyes following its path, Barney could just make out the silhouette of a small figure near the railings. The shadow stood motionless for a heartbeat, surveying the scene, and then melted away into the afternoon haze. Normality returned and the sixth-formers got into their cars. A tall, thin boy held open the car door for Gloria, but she shooed him away and climbed inside. The cars revved away in a cloud of blue exhaust fumes.

'Hey, Vice-pres!' The voice startled Barney. He looked round and saw Gabby standing beside him, a large parka with a fur-lined hood draped over her shoulders despite the warmth of the afternoon.

'Hiya,' he replied.

'Ready to go?' she asked.

'Yes,' said Barney. 'Actually, I've just seen something pretty impossible myself.'

'Oh, yes?'

'That white bird belonging to Lewis Grome I told you about? I looked for it in his bag this afternoon, but it wasn't there. And now it's appeared out of nowhere and just attacked Gloria. You know, the editor of—'

'I know who Gloria is,' interrupted Gabby.

'Well, it attacked her just a moment ago. It gave her a good pecking and then flew off back to Lewis. She was with a bunch of sixth-formers.'

'They're her staff on the *Examiner*. If she finds out that the bird has something to do with Lewis, then he's going to find himself in the paper pretty soon. Gloria loves to print nasty stories about people she doesn't like. She's been planning a story on me for a while.'

'On you?' said Barney. 'Why?'

'Well, I'm not exactly normal, am I?' said Gabby with a sad little smile. 'I'm not into make-up and celebrities and sport and all the other rot most people are obsessed with. I'm different and that's not allowed in Gloria's scheme of things. My face doesn't fit.'

'Well, *I* think your face is brilliant,' said Barney and immediately regretted it. Why had he said that? *Idiot*. He felt his own face flush hot and red.

'Cheers, mate,' said Gabby, grinning. 'Come on. You won't believe this.'

Gabby led Barney through the streets to an old railway bridge at the very edge of the town. It was made of chipped red brick and covered in faded graffiti. Beside it was a tall corrugated-iron fence. One of its iron slats was loose. Gabby held it aside so Barney could squeeze through the gap and then followed him.

'I come here to think sometimes. I like the quiet. So what do you reckon?'

Barney didn't reply, unsure what he was supposed to be looking at. He surveyed the scene: bare ground strewn with rubble, some weeds and a few trees. In the distance he could see the church and a few of the town's taller buildings. What else was there here? A grandfather clock, some crumpled beer cans ... *Hang on.*

'What's a grandfather clock doing here?' said Barney.

'That,' said Gabby, 'is a superb question. It is easily one of the best questions I have heard for a very long time.'

'That means you don't know, doesn't it?'

'That's right, genius.'

'Don't call me that,' said Barney, thinking back to Duncan and his 'Honourable Deaths' friends.

'So what do you think?'

Barney scrunched his nose in thought.

'Someone's thrown away an old clock. Is that such a big deal?'

'There's more,' said Gabby. 'It's ticking.'

'So someone's wound it.'

'It keeps moving, too.'

'What?'

Gabby pointed to the row of dandelions alongside the clock. 'When I first noticed the clock here on Monday, it was level with the first dandelion. When I came here on Wednesday, it was level with *this* dandelion.' She pointed at one a few metres to the rear of the clock. 'Today, look where it is. Near the end of the row. It's moved again.'

'Why would someone want to keep moving an abandoned old grandfather clock?'

'That,' said Gabby, 'is another brilliant question.'

'You know what we have to do, don't you?' said Barney.

'What?'

'Well, it's simple, isn't it? We get a video

camera, set it up here overnight somewhere nice and hidden away and film whoever comes to move it.'

Gabby laughed and hugged him. 'That's a brilliant idea! You *are* a genius, Barney.'

Barney blushed. The hug was enjoyably squashy. Her hair smelt of ... what? Toffee? 'Oh, well, you know, maybe a bit ...'

'We've got a camcorder at home,' said Gabby, releasing him. 'It's a bit old and knackered, but it should do the job. I'm sure we've got a tripod somewhere, too. Come on.' She set off back towards the gap in the fence with a purposeful stride.

Barney looked at his watch. He frowned. Then he let out a gasp. 'Aw, *no*!'

Gabby stopped and turned round. 'What?'

'I've just remembered I promised Mum I'd help her shift a load of stuff tonight. Boxes and furniture in the new house. We're supposed to have it looking nice before Dad comes home from work. I completely forgot. If I'm not there, she'll only try to do it alone and injure herself. And then I'll get the blame. Sorry. Can we do this tomorrow?'

'Sure. No problem, Vice-pres. We'll go round to my place after school. But I may as well warn you now,' she said.

Barney raised his eyebrows. 'About what?'

Gabby smiled oddly. 'You don't get hay fever, do you?'

CHAPTER FIVE
The Meeting

Classroom LD1 was traditionally where many of Blue Hills High's important end-of-term exams were held. It had clean white walls adorned with cheerful posters and a large rectangular window that allowed the light from outside to stream in. These things were all intended to create a calming atmosphere, aiding learning and boosting concentration. None of this ever worked, however – it taking more than sunlight and a bit of whitewash to defuse the gut-tightening terror of exams – and a faint, ineradicable air of nausea and panic clung to the place.

Although they had no tests looming, the pupils currently occupying the room were still feeling decidedly nauseous and panicky. The *Examiner*'s Friday evening editorial meeting had that effect on its staff. Ben Todwick, the paper's photographer, ran a finger over the sparse bristles he had been cultivating on his top lip for nearly a year. With the other hand, he fidgeted with his digital camera, switching it on and off repeatedly and watching the little zoom lens pop in and out of the front with its pleasing motorised whir.

'Can't you stop that? It's driving me mad,' hissed Gemma, the paper's designer, from the opposite side of the meeting table.

Ben muttered an apology and put the camera down.

A door opened at the back of the hall and

Gloria strode in carrying a laptop. She nodded stiffly to the others and took her place at the head of the table. She opened the laptop. 'Good afternoon, everyone.'

'Good afternoon, Gloria,' said the others in unison.

There were six people at the meeting. In addition to Gloria the editor, Ben the photographer and Gemma the designer, the paper's three reporters, Anna, Kerry and Giles, were also present. With the exception of Gloria, who was only twelve, they were all sixth-formers in their late teens. Most had wanted careers in the media and had seen working on the *Blue Hills High Examiner* as practical experience that would help when they came to apply for journalism courses at university. However, most had found the experience of working for Gloria so stressful that it had put them off the media for good. They stayed with the paper only for fear of ending up the subject of one of its lurid exposés, its editor not taking kindly to disloyalty.

Everyone who had ever worked at the *Examiner* had their Gloria anecdote, some war story recounting her legendary difficulty and temper. Ben recalled a tale told to him by one of the paper's previous photographers, a girl called Jessica. Jessica had taken a playful snap of Gloria's rear one afternoon when Gloria, then in Year Seven, had been bending over in the playground to do up her sandal. Jessica showed Gloria the photograph at the next editorial meeting and suggested they run it in the *Examiner* with the caption *Our Editor Gets to the Bottom of Another Mystery*. Without saying a word, Gloria shoved her backwards off her chair, nearly fracturing Jessica's skull against a blackboard. Needless to say, Jessica never worked for the *Examiner* again.

Another tale – which had now acquired the

status of legend – suggested that the previous editor, who had been expelled from school for setting fire to a teacher's car, had actually been framed for the crime by Gloria simply so she could take his place. Sometimes staff on the paper speculated about what Gloria's upbringing must have been like to create such a personality. Others wondered if she was simply some awful freak of genetics.

A burbling electronic melody rang out. Ben recognised it instantly as the theme tune to a computer game called *Lemur Patrol*. Gloria found these editorial meetings tedious in the extreme, and, believing they required only a small part of her attention, she liked to keep herself amused during them by checking her email or playing games on her laptop. *Lemur Patrol* was a particular favourite.

'The first item on the agenda,' said Gloria, tapping away at the laptop's keys, 'is the cover price. Fifty pence is far too cheap. Have you seen the amount of pocket money kids get these days? It's ridiculous. I suggest we raise it to one pound fifty. What do you think?'

The others exchanged nervous glances.

'Well?'

The sixth-formers furrowed their brows. If they simply agreed with her, Gloria would accuse them of being 'yes-weasels', but if they disagreed, she would accuse them of being negative (or 'dream-crushers').

'I think it's a strong idea in principal,' started Anna, the chief reporter, selecting her words with care. She was a biggish girl with short dark hair. 'However, not everyone will be able to afford one pound fifty, will they? Times are hard, and our research tells us the bulk of our readership is made up of kids from less well-off families.'

Gloria sniffed, her eyes never straying from the screen of her laptop. 'Bulk would be the right word. Have you seen the size of a lot of these so-called *poor* kids? Like hippos in uniforms, some of them. No, we're raising the price. If they can afford double cheeseburger and chips every day, they can afford one pound fifty for the *Examiner*. They'll just waste less money on *Chocky-Crocky* bars. If anything, we're doing them a favour.'

'Perhaps,' said Anna, 'if we allowed the school library to keep copies of the *Examiner* for some kids to read at break times ...?'

Gloria gave a snort. 'Are you mad? This is the *Examiner*, not some normal pathetic school rag padded out with word searches, raffle results and weedy attempts at poetry. We're a professional outfit providing pupils with the juicy revelations about their peers that they demand. Let them read it for free and they'll only take it for granted.'

A second electronic melody burbled. This one came from Gloria's mobile. She retrieved it from her bag and answered it. 'One sec,' she said to the others, covering the receiver with her hand. 'I've been waiting for this. Hello? Is this Mr Thompson? I'm sorry but the current offer is completely unacceptable ...' She then launched into a lengthy negotiation with a local stationer over the price of staples.

The others sat in uncomfortable silence while she talked. Ben doodled grimly on his notepad.

After some time, her haggling concluded, Gloria ended the call and put away the phone. 'Right,' she said. 'So that's agreed. Cover price to rise to one pound fifty next issue. Good. Next on the agenda ...' Her mobile rang again. 'Wait one moment,' she told the others and retrieved the phone once more from her bag. 'Ah, hello, Derek. Yes, I'd love to run the advert for your shop, but I'm afraid our rates have increased. Sadly unavoidable. Times are hard for us all economically, I'm afraid ...'

Ben rolled his eyes and looked at his watch. He was meeting his girlfriend later. They were planning to see a band, the Restless Finger Puppets, at the

Grey Goose pub. It was supposed to be a little reward for making it through the start of another boring school year. But now he could feel the evening slipping through his fingers like sand.

After some further wrangling Gloria sealed the advertising deal and put away the phone. 'OK,' she said. 'Next item.'

'The article on the Grayling girl,' said Kerry. 'It's almost ready. Ben's got some great photos and ...'

Gloria's phone rang a third time. She gave a growl of irritation and answered it. 'Hello?' she said. 'Oh, hello, Mummy.' There was a pause. She tapped a pencil against her teeth. 'Fishfingers,' she said. 'And ice cream for afters. Thanks, Mummy. Bye bye.' She hung up and heaved a sigh, rubbing her eyes with her fingertips.

'Everything OK, Gloria?' Ben asked as lightly as he could.

Gloria ignored him. 'Item two is the story about Gabrielle Grayling. You say it's almost ready, Kerry?'

'That's right, Gloria. Ben's got some marvellous photos of her looking shifty and upset and I've gathered a large number of stories about her increasingly odd behaviour. It's going to be a great piece.'

'Will it be ready for the Sunday evening deadline?'

'Not quite,' said Kerry. 'The information's all there but it still needs knocking into shape. Quite a bit of work still to do. You did say—'

'Then knock it into shape this weekend,' interrupted Gloria. She stabbed at a button on her laptop and there was a synthesised explosion. 'Got him!' she cried victoriously. 'Stupid lemur!'

'I thought you wanted to run it the week after next?' said Kerry.

'Change of plan,' said Gloria. 'I need to go with the Grayling story this week. I've got something new planned for the issue after that. So will it be ready?'

'Something new?' said Giles. 'Does that mean you're not using my story about Mr Daventry's son? I've got interviews with everyone who saw him dropping the chewing gum. It's good work.'

'Shut up, Giles,' said Gloria.

Giles opened his mouth but then closed it again.

'The thing is,' said Kerry, wincing, 'I'm going to the Lake District tonight with my family and we're not back until Sunday evening. I won't have time. I've put aside time next week especially to do this.'

'Will you have it ready for Sunday evening?'

'The thing is—'

'Kerry,' snapped Gloria. 'You're giving me problems, not solutions. I don't want to hear that. I'll ask you one more time. Will you have the article on Gabrielle Grayling ready to run in the next issue?'

'Yes, Gloria.' Kerry sighed.

'Good.' Gloria shut the laptop with a bang that

made them all jump. 'Now look, guys,' she said. 'Scrap the rest of the agenda. I'm getting bored now and there's only one more thing I want to say.'

Ben's heart leaped. He was going to get out of there on time after all.

'The issue after this one is going to be devoted to one subject and one only: Lewis Grome. Get as much dirt as you can on him.'

Giles sniggered. 'There's enough on him as it is from what I hear.'

'Which shows how much you know,' said Gloria. 'Because his appearance and level of general hygiene have improved tremendously in the space of a couple of days. At the start of term he was the same old Grimy Grome, and in a week he's suddenly changed. Why is that? His family have no money as far as I know. So how was this transformation paid for? Find out. I want everyone on this except you, Kerry. You stick to Gabrielle Grayling.'

Giles and Anna jotted notes on their pads.

'Most importantly of all,' said Gloria, her big blue eyes cold and steely, 'find out about this white bird of his that so viciously attacked me yesterday. What is it? Where did he get it? Pound to a penny he's keeping it illegally. It's not like any bird I've ever seen. It's probably a protected species or one that's been smuggled into the country. Whatever, find out how we can have it taken away from him. And then preferably destroyed. That's where you come in, Ben.' She smiled at him.

Ben's blood froze. 'Yes, Gloria?'

'Get over to his house. Right away. I want pictures of the squalor he lives in. A full spread. If he's keeping birds in his schoolbag, he's probably got a house full of them as well. You can just imagine it. I saw a thing on the news once about an insane old woman whose house was full of sick animals she'd adopted. It was disgusting. Filth everywhere. A total health hazard. That's the sort of thing I want. Don't come back without something usable. I don't care if it takes all night. Got me?'

Ben nodded slowly and picked up his camera. The Restless Finger Puppets would have to keep for another night.

CHAPTER SIX
MRS GRAYLING

On Friday, Barney's eyes scarcely left his watch all day as he willed the hands to speed forward to three-thirty. Gabby's cryptic remark about her home had intrigued him and he was keen to discover what she meant. It amused him how much the little mystery had fired his imagination.

At first sight, it looked to Barney like any other house. It was a neat-looking, smallish semi on one of the newer estates, its small square garden and driveway enclosed by a simple wrought-iron gate and a low wall topped with paving stones. The front door was wooden and painted turquoise, a little chipped and worn perhaps, but all the friendlier for it. Delicate net curtains suspended from every window veiled the interior from the outside world, providing both privacy and an old-fashioned cosiness that Barney instantly took to. It looked like the residence of a favourite aunt or maybe a beloved grandmother, the sort of place you might come for cups of tea and illicit *don't-tell-your-parents* gifts of money.

Gabby took a key out of her bag and slid it into the lock in the front door. 'Here we go,' she said. 'It's not nearly so bad once you get used to it.'

At first, Barney saw only a dim green haze. His next impression was that he hadn't stepped into a house at all, but had somehow wandered into a forest. He goggled, dumbstruck. The smell of vegetation came at him from every angle, dank and spicy.

Gabby nodded. 'Bit of a shock at first, isn't it?'

Barney ran a hand along the nearest wall. He whistled softly. He walked to the foot of the stairs and looked up. A word occurred to him. 'Wow,' he said. That seemed to just about sum it up.

'I know,' agreed Gabby. 'I know. It is a teeny bit "wow".'

Wherever Barney looked, he saw leaves. Oak leaves, beech leaves, lime tree leaves, tiny privet leaves, big hand-like plane tree leaves; they sprang and sprouted everywhere, layer upon layer of them stitched or glued or taped to every last centimetre of every available surface in the house. The leaves were yellow and brown and even orange, but mostly, overwhelmingly, they were green – green of every imaginable shade. The leaf-covered walls were like great curtains of green that shimmered and billowed in the draught from the open front door. The leaf-strewn floor was a swishing carpet of green, the leaf-plastered ceiling a canopy of green. The stairs and banisters erupted with green, looking like the ruins of some ancient civilisation overgrown by jungle. Barney tried to think of another word to say. He couldn't. 'Wow' was still all he could manage. His brain was too busy trying to process the crazy messages it was receiving from his other senses to do much more.

A grey shape flashed before Barney's eyes, a trail of leaves on the nearest wall flapping in its wake.

'Squirrel,' explained Gabby, closing the door. 'It's become rather cheeky of late. Ignore it.'

Barney followed Gabby up the stairs, leaves hissing and crackling underfoot and his brain frothing with confusion. The upstairs landing was the same: layers of innumerable leaves had been fastened to all the walls and doors in great fluttering mosaics. Even a chair, he noticed, had been painstakingly swathed in a covering of shiny green leaves.

Gabby pushed the leaf-encrusted handle of a door and a rectangular white hole appeared amidst the leaves. Barney followed her through it and found himself in a perfectly ordinary teenage girl's bedroom. There were posters on the wall, a white fluffy carpet on the floor and a bed straining under a great conglomeration of cushions and stuffed toys. Not a leaf in sight. It was as everyday and reassuring as the rest of the house was weirdly botanical. He moved aside a small heart-shaped cushion and sat down heavily on the bed. 'Wow,' he said, noting that the word was still serving him well.

'Indeed,' said Gabby and opened the door to a large walk-in wardrobe. She knelt down and rummaged through piles of clothes and toys and other junk. 'No doubt you're wondering about the decor.'

'I'm sorry?' said Barney, only half hearing. He felt as if he was in a kind of leaf-induced trance.

'The leaves,' said Gabby as she rummaged. 'You're wondering about all the leaves. Aren't you? Please say you are.'

'Well, yes,' said Barney. 'I suppose I am a bit, now you mention it.'

'Good,' said Gabby. 'I'd be seriously freaked out if you'd taken it all in your stride. The physicist Neils Bohr said anyone not shocked by quantum theory doesn't understand it. The same could be said for my mum's taste in interior design.'

'I don't understand.'

'Good. The first step to wisdom is admitting you know nothing.'

'I must be well on the way then,' said Barney. 'Because I haven't a clue about most things these days, not just this house.'

'Aha!'

'What?'

'Found what we need. Come on. We can be out before she notices we're here if we're lucky.'

'Before who notices?'

'*Gaaaaaaaaaaby?*' called a voice from downstairs. It was high and scratchy, a piping voice, somehow broken. It put Barney in mind of an elderly mouse. There were footsteps on the stairs, swift and light, and the swishing of leaves.

'Too late,' said Gabby. 'She noticed. Just don't drink the tea, OK?'

'Tea?' said Barney.

'Yes, it's vital, Barney. We'll stay five minutes to be sociable, but under no circumstances *ever* drink my mum's tea.' Gabby emerged from the cupboard brandishing a largish camcorder and a tripod. 'Right. We're all set.'

The bedroom door opened. The woman who then entered the room did so in a kind of nervous bound. She was in her forties, tall, with wild hair and wilder eyes that darted this way and that like frightened fish. She wore an old cardigan and skirt, both of which bore stylised designs of leaves. She looked Barney up and down with a few swift jerks of her head. 'Hello,' she said in her high voice. 'We've got a visitor.'

'This is Barney, Mum,' said Gabby. 'He's a friend from school.'

Barney smiled. 'Hi,' he said. Here he felt on safe ground. People's mums liked him.

'A friend?' said Mrs Grayling with a smile. 'Are you sure?'

Gabby rolled her eyes. 'Yes, he's a friend. He's joined Geek Inc.. We're just on our way out actually . . .'

'Oh, but you do have time for a quick cup of tea, don't you?' said Mrs Grayling. 'The kettle's just boiled.'

Barney and Gabby sat on two leaf-covered chairs at a leaf-covered table in the kitchen. Mrs Grayling poured some thin, green tea from a leaf-covered kettle into two leaf-covered mugs and handed one to each of them. Barney peered into his. The mug had leaves stuck to the inside as well as the outside. The tea within had turned grey and gritty and Barney was pretty sure one of the lumps floating in it was an ant. He sniffed the steaming brew. Gabby shook her head at him and he put the mug down on the table next to hers.

Mrs Grayling opened the back door and hauled in a bulging black bin liner. 'Got these from the park today,' she explained, plonking the bin liner in the middle of the kitchen floor. 'The keeper's ever so good. He lets me take what I want. Got some right beauties in here, too.' She gave a little piping giggle. 'Here, lad,' she said to Barney. 'You can help me if you like. I'm covering a dog.'

'A dog?' said Barney in alarm. Gabby gave a chuckle.

'Oh, yes,' said Mrs Grayling. 'He's called Scamp.

He's lovely. You'll like him.' She opened the door of a leaf-swathed Welsh dresser and brought out a life-size hollow plastic model of a golden retriever, the sort that stands outside shops as a charity collecting box. The dog's head was entirely encased in a mask of glossy privet leaves. Mrs Grayling placed the dog next to the bin liner and sat down beside it on the floor. 'Found him abandoned in the park. Isn't he gorgeous?' she said.

'Oh, yes,' said Barney. 'A real beaut.'

Mrs Grayling rummaged in the pocket of her cardigan and handed him a tube of paper glue. She took out a second tube for herself and then drew out a handful of leaves from the bin liner. She smeared the leaves with the sweet-smelling white paste and began to stick them one by one to the plastic dog. Barney knelt down and took a handful of leaves. They were cool and silky to the touch. He uncapped the glue and daubed some on to a leaf.

'Where are you from, then, young man?' she asked him, her eyes flitting in disconcertingly random directions as she worked. 'You don't sound like you're local.'

'Kent,' said Barney. 'We moved here a few weeks ago.'

'Oooh. That's a long way away. That's it. You concentrate on Scamp's back. I'll do his legs. I expect you miss your friends, don't you, love?'

'Well . . .' began Barney, a little taken aback. 'We still keep in touch.'

'Yes, but it's not the same, is it, if you can't actually be with them?' said Mrs Grayling. 'How old are you? Don't worry about the tail. I've got some extra small leaves saved here for that.'

'Righto. I'm eleven.'

'Oh, you poor love,' said Mrs Grayling. 'All that moving around. It's not good for a child. Pass me that big maple leaf, please. Thank you, lad. No, no sooner have you made friends then you're leaving them again. Young Gabrielle here could do with a friend or two. She doesn't seem to have the knack, I'm afraid. People just don't *get* her.'

'*Mum!*' said Gabby. She groaned. 'It's not my fault I'm the only kid in that brain-dead place with a jot of curiosity about the infinite wonders of existence. If that makes me a freak, well, I'm happy to be one.'

Mrs Grayling laughed her piping mouse-laugh. 'You see what I mean? It's good that you've joined her club, Barney. Oh, I do like what you've done there. You've made a collar! It works well.'

Barney smiled modestly. Gabby tapped him on the shoulder and mouthed the words *Let's go*. She got up. 'Thanks for the drink, Mum. We'd better be off. Stuff to do.' She motioned to Barney to get up, too.

'Yes, thank you very much,' said Barney, rising.

'My pleasure, love,' said Mrs Grayling. She touched Barney's arm. 'Just one second,' she said. 'Got something here for you. Little treat to say thank you for your help.' She went to a leaf-covered cupboard, opened it and took out something. She brought it to him on a leaf-covered plate. It was a small rectangular object bound tightly in oak leaves. 'Penguin?'

'Erm, no thanks,' said Barney, forcing a polite smile. 'Having pizza when I get home. Don't want to spoil my appetite.'

'Put it in your pocket for later, then.'

Barney took it.

'Sorry about that,' said Gabby as they walked along the avenue. She was fiddling with the camcorder's lens, unable to meet his eye. 'It's a bit much to take in all at once – the house and Mum together.'

It was another pleasant early autumn evening. The sun was fat and low in the sky and the shadows it cast were long and giraffe-spindly. Barney was carrying the tripod over one shoulder, pleased to be helping even if it was giving him an ache. 'No worries,' he said.

'You're taking this so well.' said Gabby.

'I thought she seemed quite – well – *normal*,' said Barney. 'Despite the thing with the leaves, obviously. A bit nervous maybe, but I've met madder mothers, believe me.'

Gabby threw her arms round him. Barney froze, his heart thumping. Once again he could smell the pleasant toffee odour of her hair. Eventually, she released him and they continued walking.

'Wow,' said Barney quietly. That word again. It was always there for him when he needed it, he thought, like a reliable old friend.

'Sorry,' said Gabby. 'Didn't mean to freak you out. It's just that most people are so cruel and judgemental about Mum. The kids in town always shout things at her, try to make her cry. She's so easy to mock. But you – you were confused – as well you should be; she *is* eccentric – but you were also so *nice* to her. I've never met anyone quite as cool as you before.'

Barney spluttered. 'Me, cool? That's the most ridiculous thing I've ever heard. I'm a no one. A zero.'

'You went along with her,' said Gabby. 'You didn't make her feel stupid. I appreciate that.'

'I've got no right to make anyone feel stupid,' said Barney. 'I'm as stupid as you can get.'

Gabby laughed. 'No, you're not, Barney. You're someone of rare intelligence.'

Barney snorted. He shifted the tripod on to his other shoulder. 'Has your mum always been ... *keen* on leaves, then?'

'No,' said Gabby. 'It's quite a recent thing. Only in the past year or so. She's always been totally normal. Well, she has a bit of a dodgy heart so she has to take medicine every day for that, but otherwise nothing out of the ordinary about her. She used to work at the Ministry of Defence place, just outside town. It's where Dad works, too. *Worked*, anyway. Mum was a clerical worker. Totally normal. Then one day I came home from school and the house was full of leaves. There was Mum in the middle of it all, patiently attaching them to everything with a roll of sticky tape. She said she'd spent most of the day in the park collecting them.'

'Do you know why?'

'She was looking for one that could sing.'

'Sorry?' said Barney with a smirk. 'It sounded to me just then like you said she was looking for one that could *sing*.'

'I did,' said Gabby. 'That is what I said.'

'Ah.'

Gabby chuckled. 'She said she'd been at work as usual that morning and when her tea break came around, she went outside to sit in the grass quadrangle at the centre of the building and read her book. And that was when she saw it. A smallish leaf, she said. Beech probably, but she couldn't be sure. Slightly yellowed but otherwise unremarkable. She picked it up off the ground for no particular reason and that was when it sang to her.'

'What did it sing?'

'She's never said. Only that it was the most beautiful and extraordinary sound she had ever heard and it made her happier and sadder than anything else she had ever experienced.'

'Wow,' said Barney. 'Sorry,' he added. 'Bad habit.'

'It *did* something to her,' said Gabby. 'That experience. It changed her whole outlook on life. If a simple leaf was capable of making a heavenly sound like that, the world was obviously a far weirder and more incredible place than she had ever realised. That's an oddity if ever there was one. She loved that feeling and she wanted it to continue. So she started collecting leaves, hoping to find another that could sing. She filled the house with them. Dad left not long after that.'

'Did they get divorced?' Barney tried to imagine his own parents splitting up and failed. It seemed too big, too impossible a thing to contemplate seriously.

'He just vanished,' said Gabby. 'Walked out on us. They'd been arguing a lot anyway, but the leaves thing must have been the final straw. We haven't heard from him since.' She stopped, gave a long sigh and looked down at the ground.

It seemed to Barney that Gabby needed someone to put their arm round her and tell her things would be OK and with a sudden stab of terror he realised it could only be him. But what if he was wrong? How would she react? On an impulse, he decided to risk it. But just as he was about to move his arm, Gabby continued walking. He scampered after her, half hating himself, half relieved. 'But what happened to the original leaf?'

'It ran away after she found it at work. As if a singing leaf wasn't unusual enough, this one could run, too, apparently. That's why she sticks them everywhere. So that if one ever did sing, it wouldn't be able to run away like the other one.'

'Maybe it wasn't a leaf she found?' said Barney. 'Perhaps it was some kind of stick insect. They can look like leaves, can't they? Maybe this was one that could whistle or something?'

'That did occur to me, too. But she's positive it was a leaf.'

'It must be very odd having to live in a house like that. It must drive you mental.'

'Oh, it's not too bad,' said Gabby. 'It's sort of relaxing being around all that greenery – although it has attracted a rather bold and mischievous squirrel. I haven't asked what happens when all the leaves turn brown and die. It'll be like living in a compost heap probably. But we'll deal with that when it happens. She's still a good mum. She leaves my stuff alone. I know she's got certain ... *issues*, but she's no trouble at all and all I have to do is remember not to drink the tea she makes.'

'Does she cover her food with leaves, too?'

'All she eats is leaves. But there's nothing so odd about that.'

'Really?' said Barney. It sounded odd to him. But he was no longer sure what was odd and what was normal any more.

'There's even a word for it, you know. For people who eat nothing but leaves.'

'Is there?' said Barney. 'Crikey. I suppose psychologists must have a term for every kind of strange behaviour. What is it?'

Gabby rolled her eyes. 'Vegetarian,' she said with a grin. '*Duh.*'

They set up the camera on the tripod and concealed it in a cluster of bushes not far from the grandfather clock. Gabby told Barney that a four-hour tape recording at half speed meant they would have eight hours of footage to check the next day. They could watch it on fast forward, though, because she reckoned whatever was moving the clock should be easy to spot.

They were about to go their separate ways when they heard the scream. It was male, as shocked as it was anguished, and came from the other side of the sparse copse at the rear of the waste ground. A few starlings hopping along the ground nearby flew off in surprise. Gabby and Barney sprinted off to investigate.

Behind the few withered trees, they found a fence enclosing the small garden of an old house. A section of the fence had been flattened into the ground. A boy with long greasy hair – Barney recognised him as one of the sixth-formers Gloria had been telling off the previous afternoon – was cowering in a corner of the garden clawing at the air around him. There was blood on his cheek. His camera lay on the ground, its lens smashed. Above his head, a white shape flitted like a huge angry insect.

'The bird!' said Barney. He ran to the cringing figure and tried to shoo the darting bird away, receiving a few painful nips to his neck and arms from it in the process.

Gabby kept her distance. She stared at the bird, marvelling as it swooped and dived. 'Have you actually looked at this bird?' she called to Barney.

'What?' said Barney. 'Ow! My ear!'

'Do you know what this bird is, Barney? Have you really looked at it?'

'What? Ow! Sorry. Bit busy at the moment.'

'Oh, for heaven's sake,' said Gabby. She took off her parka and threw it into the air. The heavy coat covered the bird like a net and fell to the ground. She pounced on it like a cat.

'Cool,' said Barney. 'Good work.'

The boy with the long hair staggered to his feet. 'Tell him I'm sorry,' he mumbled. 'Tell Lewis I'm really sorry. Tell *everything* I'm sorry. Make sure he gets this.' He pressed a small metal object into Barney's hand and then raced away through the copse on unsteady legs. Barney looked at the metal object. It was Lewis's pencil sharpener.

'Here's an odd thing . . .' he said to Gabby.

'I can beat that, whatever it is,' said Gabby, still crouching on her parka. She was holding tightly on to something. 'What I've got here is not merely odd, mate. This is impossible, truly impossible! I can't quite believe what I'm looking at!'

'What is it?'

Gabby got to her feet, cupping her hands together, her fingers spread apart to form a cage, and showed him what she had caught. Inside her hands the small white bird was wriggling to free itself, vibrating its wings manically. 'Can you see what it is?' said Gabby.

Barney peered between Gabby's fingers. He frowned. And then he understood. What he saw was a shape familiar to children the world over. An elegant thing, sleek, simple and beautiful.

'I can't hold it any more,' said Gabby. 'It's hurting. It feels really odd. Sort of cold. I'm going to have to let it go.' She unclasped her hands. The paper aeroplane flew out. They watched it climb higher and higher into the unbroken blueness of the afternoon sky, its wings pulsating, until they finally lost sight of it in the sun's glare.

CHAPTER SEVEN
LEWIS

Barney looked at Gabby. She was grinning like a maniac. 'How about that?' she said. 'Did you like that?'

'It was alive,' said Barney. 'It was made of paper but it was *alive*.'

Gabby nodded. 'Wasn't it one of the most fantastic things you've ever seen?'

'I can feel a certain word coming on,' said Barney.

'Hmm. Mind if I join you?'

'Be my guest.'

'*Wow*,' they said together and then burst into laughter.

'What?' said Barney. 'How? Why? How does …? What's Lewis doing with …?'

'There you go again with the brilliant questions, Vice-pres. Do you know who that guy being attacked by the plane was?'

Barney shook his head.

'His name's Ben,' said Gabby. 'He's the photographer for the *Examiner*.'

'So what's he doing here being attacked by a paper plane?'

Gabby pointed to the broken camera lying on the ground with the toe of her shoe. 'Annoying someone by the looks of it.' She picked it up and put it in the pocket of her parka.

'Lewis?' wondered Barney. He handed the pencil sharpener to Gabby. 'Ben gave me this before he ran away. To give to Lewis. Lewis was playing with it in our science lesson today and Gloria threw it in the bin. But I saw Lewis fish it out when the lesson was over.'

'Is it definitely the same one?'

'Yes, look here. I recognise these two dots Lewis painted on it.'

'So Ben stole it from Lewis. And then Lewis's paper plane attacked him?'

'What's so special about a pencil sharpener?'

Gabby placed it in the centre of her flattened palm. It sat there motionless. 'Not much by the look of it. But let's give it back to Lewis and see what he has to say.' She went to the back door of the old house and rapped her knuckles on it. It looked as though the door had once been white, but now it was the colour of rain and matted cobwebs.

There was no reply.

Gabby knocked again.

'You think this is where Lewis lives, then?' said Barney.

She pointed at a bin standing next to the door. Barney peered into it. It was full to the top with empty *Chocky-Crocky* wrappers.

The door opened.

He was dressed in a hoodie and jeans, both freshly cleaned and pressed, his hair neatly styled. The stale odour that had previously followed him around was absent. 'Hello,' he said. His eyes were vacant but not threateningly so.

'Hi, Lewis, I'm Gabby,' said Gabby. 'And you know Barney? We're from school.'

'Yes,' said Lewis without emotion.

'I believe this is yours,' said Gabby and handed him the pencil sharpener.

The small boy's eyes lit up. He cradled the metal object in his hands. 'Thank you!' he said. 'I thought I'd lost this little one for good.'

'I wonder,' said Gabby, 'if you have five minutes? Is it OK if we ask you a few questions? Just stuff we're curious about.'

'Are you from the *Examiner* too?' said Lewis. He half closed the front door.

'No,' Gabby said quickly. 'We're from Geek Inc ... It's a school club.'

Lewis shrugged. 'Breeze on in,' he said.

Neither of them expected Lewis's house to be like this. The kitchen was large and welcoming, and stocked with what looked like a complete range of brand-new appliances: an iron, a microwave, a washing machine, a dishwasher, a set of shiny utensils hanging above a gleaming aluminium sink. Against one wall stood a big black iron stove, the door in the front was open and revealed the red-hot embers within. Barney and Gabby could feel the heat radiating from it tingling on their skin. In the centre of the kitchen was a large oak table, the wood pale and polished, surrounded by several chairs like ducklings clustered round their mother. On the floor, bottle-green tiles sparkled like new. It was like a kitchen from a television commercial, fresh and clean and friendly, and the last thing either of them would have expected to find inside the house where Lewis 'Grimy' Grome lived.

'Have a seat,' said Lewis in his flat voice. He put the pencil sharpener down on the kitchen counter and rummaged in a Tupperware container. 'I've got some *Chocky-Crocky* bars here if you want one.'

They politely declined.

Lewis took one out for himself, tearing open the wrapper with his teeth. 'I suppose you're wondering about the bird,' he said.

'It's not a bird, though, is it?' said Gabby. 'I saw it up close. It's a paper aeroplane.'

'And it's *alive*,' added Barney, feeling it wise to get involved in the conversation while he still understood what was going on.

Lewis shrugged. 'It thinks it's a bird.'

'It *what*?' said Gabby, her voice rising.

Barney had wanted to say that, too, but had not been quick enough. His brain was having trouble keeping up today. 'Can I get a glass of water?' he asked.

Lewis pointed to the cupboard the glasses were kept in. 'It acts like a bird because it *thinks* it's a bird,' he told Gabby between mouthfuls of chocolate.

'But how can a paper aeroplane *think* anything at all?' said Gabby. 'It's just made out of paper.'

'That's dead easy, man,' said Lewis. 'It—'

There was a bang and a hot coal shot out of the stove. It clipped the sleeve of Gabby's parka, melting a hole in the nylon fabric. 'Yowch!' she cried and leapt off her chair. The coal clattered to the tiled floor, where it lay smoking.

'Oh. Sorry,' said Lewis. 'It does that sometimes. Better get it before it burns the place down, I suppose.' He scooped up the coal and tossed it back into the stove. 'Are you all right?'

'Fine,' said Gabby, examining the hole in her coat. 'Gives me somewhere to put a patch. But wasn't that a bit hot to pick up? Have you burnt your hand?'

Lewis stared at his palm. 'Doesn't hurt,' he said.

'That stove seems a bit dangerous,' said Gabby. 'Where are your parents? Are they here?'

With a *crack*, another coal flew out of the stove. This one missed Gabby's face by centimetres. There was a hiss and an acrid smell. 'My hair!' she cried. 'My hair's on fire!' She batted at her hair, frantically trying to snuff out the tiny worm-like orange threads of fire spreading through her curls.

Splush. A faceful of icy-cold water slammed into her. She gasped for air, stunned, soot-streaked water running down her face. Opening her eyes, she found Barney standing in front of her holding an empty glass.

'You OK?' he asked.

'Never better,' she muttered. She took off her glasses and wiped her eyes, water dripping off her nose and chin.

'The bathroom's upstairs, first on the left, if you want to get cleaned up, man,' said Lewis, scooping up the second piece of coal. 'Then I think you two had better go. I'm a bit tired and I don't really want to answer any more questions.'

They left via the back door and walked across the patch of waste ground. The grandfather clock was striking seven, its pleasant chime merging with the hum of insects and the rattle of magpies' voices in the trees.

'OK,' said Gabby suddenly sounding very businesslike. She wrung out a still-damp length of hair. 'Let's look at what we have so far. We've got an amazing paper aeroplane with a mind of its own. We've got a strange, lonely boy who's had some kind of sudden makeover and gone from smelly scruff to best-groomed boy in Year Eight. We've got a stolen pencil sharpener that Ben the photographer was so keen to get rid of. And now Lewis's kitchen. Did you notice anything unusual about the kitchen?'

'Apart from the stove that didn't like you, you mean?'

'Apart from that. Oh, and apart from the fact that Lewis could pick up those hot coals and not get burnt.'

'Yeah, I did actually,' said Barney and smiled.

'Go on.'

'You go first,' said Barney.

'No,' said Gabby, waving a mock-stern finger at him. 'If I tell you what was unusual about the kitchen, you'll just say you noticed it, too. Come on, now's your chance to impress me with your powers of observation.'

'I guarantee you didn't notice what I did,' said Barney, 'because I noticed it when I went to the cupboard to get the glass and you don't know what I saw in there.'

'Ooh,' said Gabby delightedly. 'Maybe it is different to what I noticed. Cool. OK what I noticed was this: everything in the kitchen was really, really old.'

'Was it?' said Barney. 'I thought it all looked pretty new.'

'Exactly! It was all old but it *looked* as good as new. The dishwasher, the cooker, everything, even the microwave; it was all at least thirty years old, most of it much, much older. That kettle on the stove was an antique. We did a few lessons on industrial design in history last year, and from what I remember, the stuff in Lewis's kitchen all seemed pretty ancient to me. But somehow it looked as good as new. No wear and tear. No damage. Not even a bit of grime.'

'So maybe his parents like old stuff?'

'That brings me to another point. There are

no parents. Not in that house anyway.'

'Huh?'

'When I went to the bathroom, I had a little snoop about the place. Lewis's is the only bedroom. Apart from that and the bathroom, the upstairs rooms seem totally empty.'

'He lives on his own?'

'That's what it looks like.'

They both stood for a moment trying to work through what all these clues might mean.

'He must be psychic,' said Barney finally.

Gabby laughed. 'Ooh, that's a big fat claim, Vice-pres. Invoking the paranormal at this early stage. Care to share your evidence with the rest of the class?'

'Well, I dunno about evidence,' said Barney. 'But what I reckon is Lewis has developed a psychic ability. You know the sort of thing. He can move stuff with his mind. There's a word for it. Parthenogenesis?'

'Telekinesis.'

'That's it,' said Barney. 'So Lewis has developed this telekinesis and he can make paper aeroplanes fly just by thinking about them. And he can make coals leap out of the stove when you ask him questions he doesn't want to answer.' He snapped his fingers. '*In fact*,' he went on, 'maybe Lewis isn't even aware he's doing it. It could be linked to his emotions or something? Maybe when he gets angry or upset or stressed, it makes stuff around him move. What do you think?'

'Did you just invent that whole theory?'

'Some bits,' said Barney. He looked down at his shoes. 'But most of it I got from a book I read last year called *Poltergeist High*.'

Gabby cupped her chin. 'Hmm. It's wild and crazy and implies a whole new branch of physics for which there has never been the slightest bit of evidence, despite decades of experimentation.'

'So you don't like my theory?'

She laughed. 'I didn't say that, Barney. I quite like crazy theories. But even if Lewis being psychic might explain the plane and the coals, it doesn't help us to understand why the coal didn't burn his hand. Or all the old gear in weirdly good condition in the kitchen. And what's with his sudden makeover?'

Barney shrugged. 'That,' he said, 'is where my theory doesn't really hold up, of course.'

'Nice try, sir,' said Gabby and made a sound like a contestant's buzzer in a quiz show. 'Thanks for playing.'

'Well, do you want to know what I noticed about the kitchen?'

'Ooh, yes. Go on.'

Barney opened his schoolbag and took out a *Chocky-Crocky* bar. He showed it to her. 'The cupboard I got the glass out of was full of these. I stuck one in my bag when Lewis was distracted by the coal coming out of the stove. But look, it's not actually a bar of chocolate. The wrapper is filled with something else and resealed at the end with sticky tape. I wonder what's inside? It feels all squidgy.'

'Guess what?' said Gabby. She opened her own schoolbag and took out an identical *Chocky-Crocky* bar. The end of the wrapper was crudely taped up. 'I got this from Lewis's bathroom cabinet. It was full of them, too.'

'Weird!' said Barney. 'Shall we see what's inside them?' He started to unwind the sticky tape sealing the end of his wrapper. 'It's very strange, this stuff. All soft and squidgy, but when you squeeze, it feels sort of metallic. I—'

'Don't!' said Gabby suddenly. 'Don't open it.' Her face was suddenly serious.

'What? Why not?'

'I think it might be dangerous.'

'You think? Do you have an idea of what it is, then?'

'Possibly. I need to check with someone.'

'Should we warn Lewis? His house is full of the stuff.'

She shook her head. 'I suspect he knows what he's doing. Whatever that is. But we don't want to panic him. Come round to my house tomorrow afternoon. I should have found out more by then. Can you make it?'

'I'll be there.'

CHAPTER EIGHT
HELLO, SIR

Barney pushed the half-fishfinger around the plate with his fork. Staring down at the stubby rectangle of white flesh encrusted in garish orange breadcrumbs, he found it strange to think that this had once been a living creature that swam through the dim depths of the ocean, a living being with feelings and desires not entirely different to his own.

'Enjoying that, darling?' asked his mum, who was standing beside him, watching him eat every mouthful. 'It's not too hot, is it? Or too cold maybe? I can always pop it in the microwave. Only take a few seconds.'

Barney shrugged. 'S'all right.'

'So what did you get up to today?' asked Mrs Watkins cheerily.

A little too cheerily, Barney thought. He knew that tone. It was the one his mum had used a month ago when she had tried to convince him that the move to Blue Hills would be 'an exciting adventure for the Watkins family'. 'Oh, nothing much,' he said. 'A little hanging around. Mooching about. Chilling out. You know the kind of thing.' He hoped his use of slang would bore her and make her stop asking questions.

'Tell me about the new friend you were with this afternoon. Where does he live?'

Barney winced. If he told his mum he had been spending time with a girl, it would only provoke a flood of unwanted and embarrassing questions. As it was, he had arrived home only a couple of hours later than normal – even after prearranging this with his mum – and she was treating him as if he'd just been hauled from the bottom of a ravine by a mountain-rescue team. His mum had raised overreaction to a high art. You could mention any subject under the sun to her, Barney thought, and she could find a way to twist it into something threatening to the Watkins family and to Barney in particular.

'Not far,' he said. 'On the estate near the railway line.' He pushed the plate away. 'I think I'll just go upstairs and make a start on my homework, if that's OK.'

'Of course, darling,' said Mrs Watkins. She sniffed.

'Are you all right?' said Barney.

She made a little noise that was half-laugh, half-sob. 'Fine, darling,' she said, pulling a tissue from her sleeve and blowing her nose. 'Fine. Go on now.'

Barney got up from the dinner table and headed for the stairs.

'You're not in a gang, are you?'

'What?' He stopped and turned to face her. 'What did you say, Mum?'

'In a gang?' repeated Mrs Watkins. 'It's just that you've been terribly moody recently and now what with staying out late with people I don't know ...'

'*Late?*' said Barney. 'Mum, it's half past seven. It's not even dark yet. What are you on about?'

'I read an article,' said Mrs Watkins. 'It gave the warning signs to look out for that indicate your child might have joined a gang. Moodiness and staying out late with unsuitable new friends were on the list. If you feel more comfortable talking to your dad about it ...'

Barney snorted. 'We've just moved two hundred miles away from all of my friends. Do you think that might have something to do with me being moody?'

'But you keep in touch with them all the time, don't you? On the email and whatnot. You told me.'

'It's not the same, though, is it? Bit hard to have a game of footy when I'm up here and the goal is in Kent.'

'So you're sure you aren't in a gang, darling? You can tell me, you know. I won't judge you. We can get you help.'

'Positive,' said Barney. 'I'm positive. What's this stuff you've been reading?'

Mrs Watkins opened her handbag and took out a folded-in-half newspaper. She handed it to him. 'It came from the school when they wrote to tell us you'd been accepted.'

Barney examined it. The article was accompanied by a lurid drawing of a young girl in school uniform cowering in a gutter surrounded by, somewhat oddly, a pack of slavering wolves in baseball caps. The pages of her schoolbooks were flying away in the wind, presumably symbolic of her throwing away her education. *Gangs! Is Your Child a Member – Or a Victim?* blazed the headline. In smaller writing underneath it read: *An Informative Guide for Parents by Gloria Pickles, editor.* Barney snorted again. 'Mum, it's a load of rubbish,' he said. 'They're just trying to frighten people.'

'Hmm, there seem to be a lot of very naughty children at your school,' said Mrs Watkins. 'That newspaper's full of them.'

'Honestly, don't pay any attention. I'm going upstairs.'

'If you say so,' said Mrs Watkins. 'Just make sure you never end up in this paper, eh?'

Barney sat down at his desk and emptied his bag item by item, a ritual he performed at the end of every school day. He placed his textbooks and exercise books in two neat piles on the desk. His fingers touched something unfamiliar inside the bag. He drew the object out. It was the *Chocky-Crocky* wrapper filled with ... well, filled with whatever it was filled with, he thought. He squeezed the wrapper gently between his thumb and forefinger, feeling its odd semi-liquid consistency. The next item in his bag was his empty lunchbox. He placed that on the desk and put the *Chocky-Crocky* wrapper inside it. He looked at the wrapper thoughtfully. He would be careful, he decided. He was only going to do a spot of investigating and Gabby would approve of that, wouldn't she? There would be no spillage. There would be no danger.

He began to unpeel the coils of sticky tape that sealed the end of the wrapper.

A fat tentacle of blue liquid oozed out. The

liquid was as thick as milkshake; its surface sparkled like the slushy ice drinks he liked to buy from the newsagent. Barney watched as the thick blue gloop pooled in the corner of the lunchbox. He took a pencil from his desk-tidy and dipped the point into the liquid. He held it up to his table-top lamp, marvelling at the way the viscous stuff glittered in the light.

The tiny drop of blue liquid began to spread itself rapidly across the end of the pencil. It crept along the pencil's length, a pale blue stain seeping into the wood. Barney felt a strange shiver beneath his fingers. The pencil suddenly became icy cold and he dropped it clattering on to the desk. He stared at it.

For an instant the pencil fluoresced with an eerie blue glow. And then slowly, impossibly, the tip began to rise from the surface of the desk.

Barney's heart hammered against his chest.

It throbbed so loudly he was convinced his mum would be able to hear it downstairs.

With a smooth, unhurried motion, the pencil raised itself until it was standing upright on its hexagonal base. It wobbled momentarily, as if securing its footing, its shiny grey tip pointing straight at the ceiling, and then was still. 'Hello, sir,' it said in a small friendly voice.

Barney clapped a hand to his mouth. He was going to throw up, he knew it. Either that or he was going to pass out. His head swam with black stars. His whole body tingled, his heart felt like it was about to thump its way out of his chest like a wild animal bursting out of a flimsy cage. His lips parted to say 'wow', but there was no air in his lungs.

'I said *hello*,' said the pencil, a little louder. It bowed, bending and restraightening as easily as if it were made of rubber rather than wood and graphite.

'Hello?' said Barney in a tiny hoarse whisper.

'Is there a particular task sir would like me to carry out?' asked the pencil.

'A task?'

'Yes, a task,' said the pencil. 'Some little job sir might have in mind for me to undertake? Drawing perhaps? I am a tolerable sketch artist. My tones may not be as soft and warm as a B pencil, nor as precise and clinical as an H, but you will find I am more than capable of producing pictures in a wide variety of styles. It is in the nature of an HB pencil to be jack of all trades, is it not?'

'Um, is it?' said Barney. He was having a conversation with a pencil, he told himself. A flipping pencil!

'Naturally,' replied the pencil. 'That's why we HBs remain the most popular type of pencil in use in the world today.' It bowed again, its wooden length once more flexing and straightening with impossible ease.

'How come you can talk?' said Barney.

'That is hardly my concern,' said the pencil with what Barney thought might have been a trace of impatience. 'It is not a pencil's job to ponder such questions. My purpose is quite simply to leave graphite marks upon paper and other surfaces. That and nothing more. Are there any such marks sir wishes to be made?'

'Am I going mad?' said Barney? 'Is that it? Have I gone mental?'

The pencil leaned forward slightly. Barney had the strange feeling that it was studying him. 'I don't think so,' it said. 'Sir appears to present a rational demeanour.'

'You're like the paper aeroplane, aren't you?' said Barney, his mind whirring. 'Alive. Do you know it? It belongs to Lewis Grome.'

'I have to confess, sir, that I do not,' said the pencil. 'I have only just achieved consciousness and sir is the first and so far only other sentient being with whom it has been my pleasure to converse. I know no aeroplanes, paper or otherwise.'

Barney slumped back in his chair. 'Whoa,' he said. 'This is weird stuff.'

'Very possibly, sir,' said the pencil. 'But, and I hasten to repeat myself, is there any work that sir requires of me?'

'OK, OK,' said Barney. He reached for his rough book and opened it. 'Draw me a circle.'

'Is that all?' said the pencil.

'Is that going to be a problem?' said Barney. 'Do you want me to ask you to draw something a bit more complicated? A tiger maybe? Or a hovercraft?'

'No, no,' said the pencil with an almost imperceptible sigh. 'I pride myself on being able to carry out any task required of me, no matter how trivial. A circle sir has requested and a circle I shall draw. Any particular size while I'm about it?'

'Um, radius three centimetres,' said Barney. He grinned. He was giving orders to a pencil.

'Very good, sir,' said the pencil and lowered itself until it was flat against the desktop. A bulge appeared midway along its length, as if something had gripped it in the middle and was lifting it up. Then the point lunged forward, the rear end following and bending it double again. It looked, Barney realised with astonishment, like a caterpillar undulating across the surface of his desk. It came to rest at the edge of his rough book and then flipped its rear end upwards so that it was standing – seemingly with the finest of balance – on its point. It hopped lightly on to the exercise book and then drew a perfect circle in the centre of the page, as if guided by an invisible hand.

Barney laughed delightedly. 'Wow!' he shouted. 'Wow! Wowee! Stay there! Stay there!'

'Certainly, sir,' said the pencil and flipped itself

back on to its hexagonal base to await its next instruction.

Barney tore out of the bedroom and thundered down the stairs.

'What's that I hear?' his mum called from the living room. 'Is it a baby elephant?'

Barney skidded to a halt in the hall and picked up the phone that sat on the small desk there. He wedged it between his chin and shoulder and began to dial the number he had memorised. After a few rings, a voice answered.

'Hello?'

'Gabby? It's Barney.'

'Hey, Vice-pres. Glad you called.'

'Have I got an impossibility for you!' he said. 'It's going to totally mangle your mind! I mean *totally*!' He paused. 'What's that noise I can hear in the background?'

'Ah, yeah,' said Gabby. 'About that.' She sounded strange. Her voice was wobbly. 'It's

Scamp. You remember him? The plastic dog?'

'Scamp?' said Barney. 'Yeah, I remember.'

There was a pause. Then Gabby said, 'The thing is ... he's sort of come to life a bit.'

CHAPTER NINE
LITTLE ONE

The pencil sharpener awoke with a start, its tiny mind abuzz. It lay still for a moment, gathering its thoughts. With a high-pitched noise beyond the hearing range of most human beings, it gave a long yawn.

It was barely three centimetres in length and wedge-shaped. Once it had been a lustrous gun-metal colour, but years of handling by Lewis's grimy fingers had dulled its sheen. Now its surface was smudged with graphite and coated with minute grains of sawdust.

It slid smoothly along the length of the kitchen counter on its millions of microscopic legs, scanning the room. There was no sign of the Parent.

The pencil sharpener came to a halt by the toaster, stood on its end and tapped at the toaster's silvery flank. The toaster shuffled around on its stumpy feet to see who or what had attracted its attention. 'Yes?' it said, a little gruffly, as if interrupted during some pressing business.

'Do you know where the Parent is?' asked the pencil sharpener.

The toaster sighed, issuing a fine spray of crumbs from its bread slots. 'I have no idea,' it said. 'The Parent goes where the Parent pleases and it is not the business of a humble toaster or a – what are you?'

'A pencil sharpener,' said the pencil sharpener.

'Or a *pencil sharpener*,' the toaster continued, 'to ask questions regarding his whereabouts. I toast the bread when required. You, one must presume, sharpen the pencil or pencils, whatever they may be.'

'Fat lot of use you are,' said the pencil sharpener.

'Oi! You're nicked, mate!' shrilled a voice from behind.

The pencil sharpener spun round. Facing it was a collection of cleaning products: a plastic bottle of spray bleach, a scrubbing brush, a roll of absorbent kitchen paper and a yellow scouring sponge with a green top.

'Excuse me?' said the pencil sharpener politely.

The yellow scouring sponge slithered towards it. 'What's the point,' it said in an officious snarl, 'of us slavin' away—'

'We don't slave away,' interrupted the bottle of spray bleach in a nasal trill.

'What?' said the sponge, turning back to address its colleague.

'We don't actually *slave* away,' said the bottle of spray bleach. 'I mean, we do what we do quite willingly, don't we? No one's forcing us. So *slave* isn't really the right word to use. It gives the wrong impression.' The other cleaning products murmured in agreement.

'I don't believe I asked for your opinion,' said the sponge.

'Well, no' started the bottle of spray bleach. 'But—'

'Then kindly refrain from stickin' it in where it isn't wanted,' said the sponge. 'It was just a figure of speech, all right? No need to make a big thing out of it.'

'Pardon me for living, I'm sure,' said the bottle of spray bleach.

'Now look here,' said the sponge, turning back to the pencil sharpener. 'As I was saying, what is the point of us slav—that is *workin'* all the hours of the day tryin' to keep this place clean and tidy if you're going to spoil it all by hangin' around the kitchen surfaces lookin' all scruffy and leavin' dirty marks and sawdust everywhere you go, eh? I mean, what is the point?' With a corner, it gestured to a thin, dirty smear a little like a snail's trail that the pencil sharpener had left in its wake as it had scuttled across the counter.

'I don't know,' said the pencil sharpener. 'What is the point?'

'The point,' said the sponge, 'is that I and my team here have got better things to do all day than clean up after the likes of you. And I believe I would be well within my rights to stick you down the waste disposal and grind you into bits. What do you think of that, eh?'

'I don't want any trouble,' said the pencil sharpener. 'I'm looking for the Parent. Have you seen him?'

'The Parent?' said the sponge, rearing up on to its edge and towering menacingly over the tiny pencil sharpener. 'You stay away from him.' The pencil sharpener squeaked and retreated, bumping its rear against the toaster. 'The Parent,' said the sponge, 'is not to be bothered by an insignificant little—'

'We really haven't, you know,' interrupted the bottle of spray bleach again.

'What?' hissed the sponge, flopping back on to the counter.

'We really haven't got anything better to do than clean up,' said the bottle of spray bleach. 'That's what we're meant to do after all. We're cleaning products.'

The others agreed. 'I actually quite enjoy it,' chipped in the scrubbing brush.

'Enjoyment don't enter into it,' said the sponge. 'I'm not interested in what you do or don't enjoy. Keepin' the house and its contents clean is our job and if this scruffy article,' – it waved a corner at the pencil sharpener – 'is determined to dirty the

place up, then we had better do somethin' about it sharpish.' It leered at the pencil sharpener. 'It's the waste disposal for this little one. No doubt about it.'

'Have you ever thought,' said the bottle of spray bleach in its nasal voice, 'that if it wasn't for things like this pencil sharpener bringing dirt in here, we'd be out of a job? The Parent wouldn't need us at all. If anything, we should be grateful to the little chap for providing work for us. What do you think of *that*?'

'He's right,' muttered the kitchen roll. 'A world without dirt is a world with no need for cleaning products.' This brought a loud chorus of agreement from its fellows.

'Are you lot mad?' said the sponge. 'You actually want dirt?'

'Don't get me wrong,' said the bottle of spray bleach. 'I like a clean surface as much as anyone, but for me it's the *process* – the cleaning itself –

rather than the end result that gives me the most satisfaction.'

'Good point,' said the scrubbing brush. 'What I like to do is scrub things. When something's *been* scrubbed, I tend to lose interest in it.'

'I can't believe I'm hearin' this,' said the sponge.

'I'm just putting the idea out there for discussion,' said the bottle.

'I don't care,' said the sponge. 'This ain't a debatin' club. This is the Parent's kitchen and I'm in charge of keepin' it spick and span and if I say this dirt-carryin' little runt is going in the waste disposal, into the flamin' waste disposal he flamin' well goes. You with me? Or do I have to take this up with the Parent? Cos I will, you know. He listens to me. Just try me. I dare you.'

The scrubbing brush started to say something, but then decided against it. 'Yeah, yeah,' it sighed. 'Whatever you say.'

'Don't worry,' said the bottle of spray bleach quietly to the brush. 'We'll have a meeting about this later.' It lowered its voice to a whisper. 'When the sponge has his nap.'

'Right,' said the sponge. 'Glad to see we've got that sorted out. Now I believe before I was interrupted I was about to cast this grimy little trespasser into the waste disposal '

But when it turned back, the pencil sharpener was nowhere to be seen.

'He appears to have gone, sir,' said the bottle of spray bleach.

'I can see that, thank you very much,' said the sponge. 'Good, then. I obviously scared it away. It'll think twice before dirtyin' up *this* place in a hurry.' With a swift movement, it wiped away the smudgy trail that the pencil sharpener had left behind. 'Right, lads, I can see a thin layer of dust formin' on the seat of that chair over there. Follow me.' It slithered off across the counter and then slid down the side of the washing machine. The others followed.

When they had gone, a small metallic shape hauled itself out of one of the toaster's bread slots and clambered back on to the surface of the kitchen counter. 'Thanks for letting me hide,' said the pencil sharpener. 'Sorry I snapped at you earlier.'

'You're welcome,' said the toaster. 'Anything to annoy that brainless sponge.'

As the pencil sharpener slid through the doorway, it became aware that it was entering an entire new ecosystem. A human observer would have thought it more like a coral reef than a child's bedroom. The pencil sharpener halted, fatigued after its ascent of the stairs, and watched as hordes of objects bustled about the place, each intent on its particular task.

Beneath the window stood an ironing board

and on it an iron was propelling itself across Lewis's school shirt. Next to it on the floor his crumpled school trousers, jumper and various items of underwear queued patiently for their turn. The iron slid off the shirt and gave a snort of steam. The shirt climbed down and folded itself neatly on a chair beside the bed. Now the trousers clambered on to the ironing board. Nearby, on a small rickety desk, a biro was busy writing an essay in Lewis's English book, while a pencil and set square laboured over his maths homework, occasionally consulting a calculator. Beside the bed a stout brush was applying sticky black polish to Lewis's shoes.

The pencil sharpener slithered up the leg of the desk to get a better view. It surveyed the room. There was the Parent! He was dozing on the bed, surrounded by a gaggle of objects that were fussing over him. A tiny set of silver scissors was trimming his fingernails, carefully catching the clippings and depositing them in a small porcelain ramekin that trundled obediently behind. A pair of white cotton buds cleaned his ears while a comb ran itself through his hair, walking on its rippling, spindly teeth like a tall, thin centipede. The bed's blankets hugged him in their swirling embrace, the pillows plumping themselves comfortably around his head.

The Parent opened his eyes. He saw the pencil sharpener and held out his arms in welcome. 'Little one!' he cried delightedly.

The pencil sharpener leapt on to the bed and bounded towards Lewis, all thoughts of tiredness banished from its mind.

CHAPTER TEN
ORVILLE MCINTYRE

'Remarkably perky for a creature made of plastic, isn't he?' said Gabby. They watched as Scamp padded about Gabby's bedroom, sniffing curiously at everything, his hollow tail wagging with pleasure and glinting in the morning sunlight streaming in through the window.

Barney blinked in astonishment. 'Wow.'

'That's not all,' said Gabby. 'Listen.'

Barney listened. He heard nothing. 'What—?'

'Sssh!' hissed Gabby, pressing a finger to her lips.

'*Status undetermined,*' said a voice.

'What was that?' said Barney.

'Scamp,' said Gabby. 'Every couple of minutes he says "status undetermined".'

'Why?'

'Haven't the foggiest!'

'How come his head's still got leaves all over it?' said Barney. 'Doesn't that make it a bit hard to see where he's going?' He sipped his tea, thankful that the mug was one of Gabby's own and not plastered with leaves.

'Apparently not,' said Gabby. 'Look at him. He seems to get about all right. It's ... *well–*'

'A little bit impossible?' suggested Barney.

'You said it, Vice-pres. But at least we know what brought the paper plane to life. It's this blue squidgy stuff Lewis is storing in his chocolate wrappers. I know I said it might be dangerous, but I couldn't help myself having a poke about in it yesterday after you left.'

Barney grinned. 'Couldn't resist it, eh?

'That stuff is seriously weird. Imagine if it had splashed everywhere! The whole house might be alive!'

Scamp trotted up to Barney, panting lightly. Barney went to pat him.

'Status undetermined,' said Scamp.

'Don't,' said Gabby. 'He's really cold. It hurts to touch him for long. I don't know why.'

'Ah, of course,' said Barney.

'What do you mean, "of course"?'

'Confession time,' said Barney. He reached into his coat and drew out his pencil case from an inside pocket. Gabby looked at him quizzically. He unzipped the pencil case and took out a pencil. He placed it on the bed next to Gabby, who was sitting beside him. 'Say hello,' said Barney to the pencil.

The pencil twitched into life. It sat up, bending in the middle in its impossible way, tip pointing upwards. Gabby gasped. 'Good morning,' it said. 'Does sir or madam have a task they require carrying out?'

'It ... it—!'

'Talks?' said Barney nonchalantly. 'Oh, yeah. He talks properly. Seems to bend like rubber, too, even though he's wood. No idea how he does that. He draws, of course. Anything I want.'

'No,' said Gabby. 'I thought Scamp was going to totally freak you out this morning. But then you introduce me to a talking pencil. Ha, I'm glad I let you join Geek Inc., Barney. You're weirder than I am.'

'Excuse me,' said the pencil. 'Will I be needed?'

'Whoops,' said Barney. 'He seems to get a bit tetchy if he feels you're wasting his time.' He picked up the pencil and placed it back in his pencil case. 'No drawing required just at the moment, thank you.' He closed the case's zip.

'Crazy,' said Gabby. She flopped back on the

bed and stared up at the ceiling. 'Crazy, crazy craziness. I love it!'

'What do you think is in this blue stuff that makes things come to life?'

'I have a vague idea,' said Gabby. She looked at her watch. 'In fact, we're shortly going to meet up with someone who might be able to tell us all about it. But before we do, look at this.' She slid off the bed and turned on a small portable television that stood on her dressing table. Barney saw that it was connected by a cable to Gabby's camcorder. Snowy fuzz appeared on the screen. Gabby hit a button on the camcorder and an image appeared showing the lonely grandfather clock standing in its patch of waste ground. 'Check this out,' she said. 'Fast forward.' She hit a button on the camcorder and two bars of interference appeared on the screen. Clouds raced across the sky behind the grandfather clock and the daylight began to fade with unnatural speed. After a moment, with slow, rocking steps, the grandfather clock waddled forward a few metres. Then it was still again, as if fatigued from its exertions.

'Mystery blue stuff does it again?' said Barney.

'But why's it moving so slowly?' said Gabby.

Barney shrugged. 'Maybe it's old?' Just then Scamp bounded up to them. 'What does your mum think about the "new" Scamp?' he asked.

'She doesn't know yet,' admitted Gabby. 'She was asleep last night when he came to life, and when I woke up this morning, she'd gone out. She often does that. Goes out early to the park usually to collect leaves.'

'Hmm ... speaking of leaves. What if we tried to use the blue stuff to bring a leaf to life? You could see if it sings,' said Barney. He suddenly laughed.

'What?' said Gabby.

'I bet no one in the history of the world has ever said that sentence before.' He went to take a sip of tea and as he did so, Scamp suddenly jumped on to the bed beside him, unbalancing him. He dropped the mug, splashing hot tea along Scamp's back.

'*Status undet . . .*'

The plastic dog froze abruptly and fell on to the bed, silent and still. 'Scamp?' said Barney. He nudged the animal. Scamp did not respond.

Gabby took hold of Scamp's foreleg. It was stiff. She rapped at the dog's side gently with her knuckle. Scamp was completely immobile once more, a hollow lifeless charity collecting box. 'The effect's stopped,' she said. 'The hot tea must have cancelled it out somehow.'

'Sorry,' said Barney. He took a tissue from his pocket and began to mop up the spilt tea staining Gabby's duvet. 'I'm such a clumsy fool.'

Gabby smiled. 'No, Barney, you're quite the reverse.'

The interior of the OK Café was almost as hot and humid as a sauna. Tinny music from an ancient radio merged with the chatter of customers, the clatter of cutlery against plates and the crackle and hiss of frying food. The proprietor, a tall, thin man with a long, dejected face, was scooping hot fat over the yolk of an egg with a spatula when Barney and Gabby entered. He watched as they peered around the crowded café and then went to sit at a table opposite a plump young man wearing a checked tweed suit. The proprietor didn't approve of kids in his café. They were noisy, in his experience, disturbing the other customers and rarely buying more than one can of pop.

The man in the checked suit called over to him. 'One can of orangeade for my young friends to share, please.'

The proprietor grimaced and opened the door of his chiller cabinet. He took out a can, found two clean glasses and brought them over. The man thanked him. The proprietor hurried back to his egg.

'Thanks for agreeing to meet us,' said Gabby, pouring some orangeade for herself and Barney.

'Not at all, not at all,' said the man in the checked suit. 'Simply super to see you again, Gabby. It really is. Who's your friend?'

'Barney,' said Gabby.

'Hello, Barney,' said the man. He gave Barney a warm smile and a hearty handshake. He looked about twenty-five, his face round and red and jolly. When he spoke, his voice was rich and fruity, reminding Barney of the voice-over from a television cake commercial.

'This is Orville,' said Gabby to Barney. 'Orville McIntyre. He used to work with my dad at the Ministry of Defence.'

At the mention of Gabby's father, McIntyre shifted uncomfortably in his seat. 'No word from him, then, I take it?' he asked softly.

Gabby shook her head.

McIntyre made a sympathetic noise. 'I'm so sorry to hear that,' he said. 'Such a remarkable man, your father. A great loss to us, involved, as he was, in so many ... *well* ...' His voice trailed away. For a second he seemed embarrassed. Then he smiled warmly. 'How's your charming mother dealing with it?'

'She's coping,' said Gabby. 'In her own way.'

McIntyre beamed. 'Excellent! I'm sure this is just some temporary problem he's coping with. No doubt your father will be back in touch when he's ready.' Gabby didn't look convinced. 'So what is it that I can do for you today?'

Gabby reached into her bag and took out a plastic flask decorated with kittens and flowers. McIntyre looked at it with a bemused expression. Gabby unscrewed the top and poured a measure of the stodgy blue liquid from it on to a saucer. 'What can you tell me about Artificially Intelligent Non-Newtonian Fluids?' she asked.

The colour drained from McIntyre's face. 'Where the hell did you get this?' he hissed. He snatched up the saucer and hurriedly poured the contents back into the flask, shooting nervous glances around the café. Barney noticed that his hands were shaking. 'I'm going to have to take this,' said McIntyre. 'It's toxic. I can't let you keep it.' He turned to Barney. 'Have you got any?'

Barney took the *Chocky-Crocky* wrapper from his inside pocket and showed it to him. McIntyre grabbed it. He pulled a leather briefcase out from under the table and put the wrapper and Gabby's flask into it.

'So what is it?' asked Gabby.

McIntyre ignored her question. 'Where did you get it?'

'Tell us what it is,' replied Gabby. 'Or we won't tell you anything.'

'You don't understand,' said McIntyre in an urgent whisper. His face was hard as iron now, all

traces of jolliness gone. 'This isn't a game. This is government business. I'm afraid you two are completely out of your depth here.'

No change there, thought Barney.

'Dad never spoke too much about his work,' said Gabby. 'He wasn't allowed. But one day, not long before he vanished, he left the memory stick on the kitchen table by accident. I thought it was one of mine, but when I plugged it into my computer, I saw that it was full of document files, including one describing something called Artificially Intelligent Non-Newtonian Fluids. The files were about computers made of weird stringy liquids instead of metal and microchips and stuff. That's what this blue stuff is, isn't it? A new type of computer. That's how it can bring things to life. It creates an artificial intelligence in objects somehow.'

'Bring things to life?' said McIntyre. He smiled pleasantly. 'What fanciful rubbish. I'm sure I have no idea what you're talking about.'

Barney reached into his inside pocket and drew out the pencil. He balanced it on its end on the table. 'Hello, sir,' it said in its friendly voice. 'Am I required?' McIntyre gasped and made a grab for it, but Barney was too quick and snatched the pencil away, placing it back inside his coat. McIntyre's eyes flicked around the café once more, making certain that they were not being observed.

'Do you know what we're talking about now?' said Gabby cheerfully.

The green of the grass in the park was so intense in the late morning light that Barney could not look at it without squinting. Each shimmering blade seemed daubed with a radioactive brilliance. He shaded his eyes with his hand, wishing he owned a pair of sunglasses.

They were strolling along the narrow central path that bisected the park into two large tree-lined fields. On one side of them a game of football was in progress and boys of nine and ten were scrabbling furiously and demanding that they be passed the ball, each team composed, it seemed, of eleven star strikers. On the other side younger children and their parents fed handfuls of stale bread to ducks on a small oval pond, shooing away the little crowds of pigeons that gathered to scavenge the crumbs.

When they reached the centre of the park, Orville McIntyre halted and raised his hand. 'This should do us,' he said. 'We won't be overheard here.' He took out a pipe and thumped its bowl against the side of a nearby bench to empty it. He filled it with tobacco and lit up. 'Now,' he said, puffing, 'I want you to tell me everything.'

Gabby shook her head. 'You first. Tell us what this stuff is. Tell us what we've found.'

McIntyre sighed, exhaling a puff of blue-white smoke from each nostril. 'It seems I must,' he said.

'Very well.' He sat down on the bench and crossed his legs, glancing around furtively.

'So tell us about the blue gunk,' said Gabby.

'You were quite right, Gabby,' said McIntyre. 'This "blue gunk" as you call it is indeed what we call an Artificially Intelligent Non-Newtonian Fluid.'

'Is this what Dad was working on?'

'Yes,' said McIntyre. 'And me, too. I daresay you're aware of the field of nanotechnology?'

'Sure,' said Gabby.

Barney frowned. 'I'm not.'

'It's the ultimate in miniaturisation,' said Gabby. 'Making machines out of atoms and molecules. That's right, isn't it?' She looked at McIntyre.

'Bang on,' said McIntyre. 'And it's one of the most exciting areas of current science. Your father and I were engaged on a project connected with so-called "smart weapons", that is to say, weapons which contain a certain amount of computer technology and can to some extent think for themselves.'

'What, like a bomb that asks you your name before it blows you up?' said Barney with a smirk.

'That's more or less exactly it,' said McIntyre. 'Yes.'

'What?' said Barney. 'That's ridiculous. I was joking. You wouldn't make a bomb that did that, would you?'

'Be a lot better than a bomb that blows people up regardless of who they are, wouldn't it?' said McIntyre with a wry smile. 'Anyway, nanotechnology. Gabby, your father and I were tasked with creating a new strain of these smart weapons. Our backgrounds are both in computer science, of course, specifically the field known as AI – artificial intelligence. That's where you try to build and program computers to emulate the workings of the human mind – to be responsive and conscious, like a living organism and not just a glorified pocket calculator. Through our research we came to realise that computers need no longer be bulky metal objects that sit on desks. Using nanotechnology, we were able to build them as minutely thin but immensely long microscopic chains, a little like the DNA molecule itself. When we combined millions of these chains, they formed themselves spontaneously into a liquid computer of immense power. It was what we call a non-Newtonian liquid because it behaves in rather odd ways, unlike, say, water, whose properties are quite simple to understand.

'Now what all this meant was we could coat a weapon with a thin layer of this liquid and effectively turn it into a hugely powerful computer. The idea was we would have smart missiles that knew exactly where they were supposed to be going, and avoid blowing up civilian targets by accident. Or a bullet that you could fire randomly into a crowd and be sure that it would hit only the one person you had intended it to. But it required a heck of a lot of work. We spent ages, simply ages, working out the behaviour patterns of the various pieces of weaponry which would receive the coating of liquid – and then we had our brainwave: instead of creating a new and unique kind of liquid computer for every piece of weaponry we needed to coat, we could make just one type – but give it the ability to recognise whatever it coated. It was a stroke of genius, in a way.'

'Um, can you explain that all again in a way that two people who haven't even done GCSE science yet might understand?' said Gabby.

'Yes, please do,' said Barney. He was annoyed to find that he had been staring at a clump of leaves in the distance and only half listening to what McIntyre had been saying and was now completely lost.

McIntyre puffed on his pipe. 'Basically, we

created a single kind of liquid computer. We were going to called it *The Elixir of Prometheus* after the Greek god who stole fire from Zeus and gave it to man. Because it puts the spark of life into anything it touches. But everyone thought it sounded too pretentious so we settled on the name *Technoslime* instead.'

'Technoslime?' said Gabby. 'It's catchy. I like it!'

McIntyre guffawed. 'Its name was the least of our problems. The stuff worked like this: each tiny chain was able to connect wirelessly to the Internet and find information about whichever object it was in contact with, not just bullets and missiles but anything that could be of benefit to a soldier from becoming "smart" – guns, pens, toothbrushes – literally anything.'

'Toothbrushes?' asked Barney. 'What use is a living toothbrush?'

'Anything that saves a soldier time and energy is useful when in combat,' said McIntyre. 'It can mean the difference between life and death. So, when a drop of Technoslime touched an object, it immediately identified it and assigned skills and capabilities to it accordingly. In this way a pen would develop the ability to write under its own power, like your pencil there. A gun would be able to identify and fire at its own targets – and so on. To go with this we developed a user-friendly interface that was, even if I say so myself, frankly brilliant.'

Gabby raised her eyebrows. 'Oh, yes? And what was that?'

'A personality. When an object came into contact with Technoslime, it developed a personality – a will of its own connected to its purpose as an object. We made guns that actively *wanted* to fire. Missiles that yearned to blow things up. Rather than have our soldiers waste valuable time programming their commands into each item, we made the objects respond to spoken commands and gave them the ability to speak back. It really does make things come alive.' He pointed his pipe at Gabby. 'Have you heard of something called imprinting?'

Gabby frowned. 'I think we did that in biology – something to do with baby birds?'

McIntyre nodded. 'When a bird such as a duckling hatches from its egg, it *imprints* on the first living thing it sees, that is, it—'

'It thinks the first thing it sees is its mother and follows it everywhere,' Gabby finished for him.

'Spot on.'

Barney guffawed. 'So my pencil thinks I'm its mother?'

'What's the matter?' said McIntyre with a wry smile. 'Do you have some objection to being the single parent of an item of stationery?'

'It doesn't act like I'm its parent,' said Barney. 'It seems a bit snippy, if anything.'

'You'd be surprised how some people treat

their mothers,' said McIntyre and Barney suddenly felt himself blush. He turned away from the others and strolled off to look at the clump of leaves he'd been staring at before. 'The thing is,' McIntyre went on, 'there were severe unintended consequences to the creation of Technoslime which meant it could never actually be used. First, for such complex nanotechnology to function efficiently Technoslime must keep itself at a very low temperature.'

'So that's why the animated objects are always freezing to the touch,' said Gabby.

'Not much good to the soldier if his smart new kit is too cold to pick up,' said McIntyre with a snort. 'But secondly, and far more importantly, it turned out that there was a certain unpredictability – a randomness – to the types of personalities objects would develop. Something to do with chaos theory apparently. Sometimes we'd bring a rifle to life only to find it was actually a pacifist! Not much use in a battle situation, I'm sure you'll agree. Other times we'd bring an object to life and find that the only thing it wanted to do was sing and dance. It was quite ridiculous.'

Gabby and Barney exchanged a wild-eyed stare. Gabby mouthed the word *Mum!*

'In the end the entire project was abandoned and the MOD's whole stock of Technoslime was meant to be incinerated. Gabby, you have to tell me where that missing container of it is.'

'Won't it be running around somewhere with a mind of its own?'

McIntyre shook his head. 'Technoslime is only effective in single droplets. In large amounts the effect is cancelled out. We have to find it, my dear, otherwise—'

'Gabby! Gabby!' It was Barney. He was calling over to her from the clump of leaves, frantically waving his arms.

'What is it?'

'Come quick!'

She raced over to him. Barney was kneeling down, scrabbling through the leaves with his hands. 'What's wrong?' said Gabby. 'What have you found?'

'Call an ambulance,' said Barney. 'On your mobile. Do it now.'

'What?'

'Look.'

Gabby stared at the pile of leaves. Something suddenly struck her as odd. Some of the leaves ... they *weren't* leaves. They were pictures of leaves. Pictures on fabric: a skirt and jumper with leaf designs woven into them. An ice-cold spear of terror pierced her heart. 'No,' she muttered. 'No, no.' She clawed desperately at the loose leaves and uncovered something white, something shockingly familiar. A face.

'I'm sorry,' said Barney. 'It's your mum.'

CHAPTER ELEVEN
THE SPY

Gloria ran a hand across the railings, the metal smooth and cool under her fingers. The night was still and clear, the sky dusted with faint stars. A car engine droned and she saw the yellow-white glare of its headlights illuminate the underside of the railway bridge. Thrusting her hands into her pockets, she put her head down and walked a few paces along the pavement. The car passed. She returned to the railings, feeling each slat in turn, testing for ... *ah*. There it was.

She slid aside the loose slat and climbed through the gap.

Ben's garbled, half-hysterical phone call about Lewis's house being 'alive' had made no sense whatsoever. What had he said? He'd been attacked by a stove and chased away by a gang of chairs? It was ludicrous, like something out of a nursery rhyme. To compound this idiocy, he had told her he had lost his camera, and along with it any photographic evidence of the state of Lewis's house. He had obviously cracked under the strain of working for the *Examiner*. He wasn't the first and he wouldn't be the last. Yet some unmistakable tone of sincerity in his voice had nagged at her, suggesting there was something worth investigating going on there after all.

Whatever. She would find out for herself. It was pointless delegating truly important tasks to others. They could never be trusted.

In the distance lay the rectangle of light that marked Lewis's kitchen. Gloria headed for it, stumbling every now and then over a pothole or broken brick. A tall shape reared up in front of her. She gasped, throwing up her hands to protect her face, her blood freezing in her veins. The shape towered over her, motionless. It looked like some kind of large post or obelisk. There was a metal plaque attached to the front with numbers on it. Gloria snorted in relief. Someone had dumped on old grandfather clock here in the middle of this waste ground. She felt half inclined to push it over, anticipating the delicious crash as it shattered against the concrete, but knew this would only attract attention. Instead, she hurried past it, making for the flattened patch of wire fencing at the edge of Lewis's garden.

Years before, when Gloria was at primary school, aged six, she had gone looking for her friend

Lindsay one playtime and found her huddling in a far corner of the playing field with five or six other children. They were all hunched over a large cardboard box, whispering and giggling. 'What's going on?' Gloria asked.

Lindsay spoke in a breathless rush. 'The van came with new stuff for the tuck shop, but the man didn't want to wait for Mr Hoyle to get it so he left it on the step and Ethan took it and brought it here and now everyone's helping themselves!'

Helping themselves was right. The children had ripped the lid off the box and were filling their schoolbags and coat pockets with chocolate biscuits, packets of crisps, cartons of drink and other treats in a frenzy of guilty pleasure. What struck Gloria as odd was that the children who were participating in this act of pillage were not the ones who were usually naughty. They were all sensible children and what her mother would describe as 'well brought up'.

'Here,' said Lindsay, pressing a chocolate bar into her hand. 'Take one. It's free!'

'But you'll get in trouble,' said Gloria, doubt in her voice.

'Nobody will find out!' said Lindsay.

Gloria stared at the *Chocky-Crocky* bar that her friend had given her doubtfully, and then back at the other children who were still grabbing as much of the loot as they could. She slipped the bar into the pocket of her school cardigan.

When the box had been emptied, Ethan chucked it over the fence into a hedge in the bowling green that backed on to the school playing field, hiding the evidence of the crime. The bell rang signalling the end of morning playtime and the children trooped inside, giggling at their own boldness.

Later that morning Gloria's form teacher, Miss Coleman, sent her off to the art supplies room to fetch a pack of sugar paper. Gloria was always entrusted with these errands, the teachers considering her an efficient and reliable girl. When she arrived at the storeroom, she went inside, turned on the bare-bulb light and closed the door. She sat on a rubber-topped metal library stool and took out the *Chocky-Crocky* bar from the pocket of her cardigan. She stared at the garishly wrapped bar for several seconds, imagining its rich creamy texture. Then she put it back in her pocket. She took a pack of sugar paper from a shelf and turned out the light. But, instead of going back to her classroom, she went the opposite way up the corridor and knocked on the door of the head teacher's office.

'Come in,' said a cheerful voice.

Gloria went inside.

'And what can I do today for Miss Gloria Pickles?' said Mr Roberts the head teacher, his eyes scarcely leaving his paperwork. He was a short, curly-haired man with a jowly face.

Gloria put on a serious expression. 'I need to report a crime, sir.'

'A crime?' said Mr Roberts, looking up at her with his full attention now. 'Goodness me. What's happened?'

'Ethan Rogers stole the box with the tuck-shop supplies that the man delivered this morning. He and some other children opened it and took all the stuff that was inside.'

'No! Really? Are you sure?'

'I saw them, sir. Simon Carr, Susan Taylor, Hannah Edwards, Robert Hughes and Lindsay Spear. They all took things. They put them in their bags and in their pockets. Then Ethan threw the box over the fence.'

Mr Roberts jotted down the names as she spoke. 'I see,' he said. 'You're good friends with Lindsay Spear, aren't you?'

'I am, sir,' said Gloria. She looked at her shoes. 'The thing is, Lindsay gave me one of the chocolate bars she had stolen. I think she wanted me to be in on it, too, so we'd both get into trouble. But I never want to get into trouble, sir.' She took the *Chocky-Crocky* bar from her pocket and placed it on Mr Roberts's desk. 'I always want to do the right thing, sir. If you see someone being naughty, you have to tell on them, don't you? Or you're just as bad as them. Even if you're friends with them. Even if you think your friends will get their own back on you, you have to do it. That's what Miss Coleman told us.'

Mr Roberts nodded gravely. 'Indeed, my girl. That's right. But don't worry about Lindsay and the others finding out. They'll never know it was you who told me. Thank you for coming to me today, Gloria. You did the right thing.'

Gloria smiled modestly. 'I have to take this sugar paper to Miss Coleman.'

'Of course. Off you go.'

Gloria strolled back to class. Lindsay wasn't

that much of a friend, she reflected. She was just a girl she hung around with sometimes. Gloria didn't have any real friends. She found other people slow, wearisome.

The children cut the sugar paper into shapes and stuck them on to pieces of white card to create collages. 'What artists do when they make pictures,' Miss Coleman told them, 'is try to tell the truth. They try to find something true about the world and show it in their art. Think about that when you're making your collages.'

The class worked in contented silence, everyone concentrating on their work, but before very long, a child from another class brought a note to Miss Coleman. She read it twice, and then spoke to her class in an official-sounding voice. 'Ethan Rogers, Simon Carr, Susan Taylor, Hannah Edwards, Robert Hughes, Lindsay Spear – please go to Mr Roberts's office now.'

The named children got to their feet. Some

started to cry. The game was up. The others in the class exchanged glances, curious and a little alarmed, wondering what trouble their classmates were in.

When the lesson was nearly over, Miss Coleman collected the collages that the class had constructed. Many children had made forests and flower shapes. One boy had made a miniature zoo populated by lots of tiny animal shapes. He had given all the animals sad expressions because he said they didn't like being locked up in their cages. Miss Coleman liked that. Then she saw Gloria's collage. 'What have we here?' she asked her. 'It looks a bit like a newspaper.'

'That's what it's supposed to be, miss,' said Gloria. 'It's the front page. Mr Roberts gave me an exclusive – that's what you call it when someone tells their story to you only.' Miss Coleman chuckled. Gloria had cut black sugar paper into blocky capital letters and stuck it to the white card to create the effect of a newspaper article with a bold banner headline. She held it up for Miss Coleman and the rest of the class to read.

'TUCK SHOP THEFT SHAME OF MiSS COLEMAN'S CLASS,' it said. 'ETHAN, SiMON, SUSAN, HANNAH, ROBERT AND LiNDSAY TO BE PUNiSHED BY HEADTEACHER TODAY.'

'What's this?' said Miss Coleman sharply.

Gloria laughed. 'It's what you wanted, miss,' she said. 'It's the truth.'

The truth, thought Gloria as she peered round a tree at the darkened garden, what a powerful weapon it was. If you could discover it, you could use it to control people's lives – ruin them if you wanted. Whoever said 'The truth will set you free' must have been having a right old laugh.

Keeping low, she crept along the wall of the house until she was underneath the window. She held on to the sill, her small hands strong and purposeful, and slowly raised herself just enough to peep through into the kitchen,

What she saw made her gasp, made her huge blue eyes widen in fear and astonishment. She felt her heart drum against the inside of her chest.

Lewis was sitting at the kitchen table eating a meal while all around him a seething swarm of living objects fussed and trundled. A pair of mops processed along the floor, cleaning it with great swishing steps as they marched. Beyond them a draught excluder looking like a fat woollen snake slithered to cover the crack beneath a door. On the table a silver teapot poured its contents into a mug which bowed to receive the steaming brew. A jug waddled up and added milk while a pair of sugar cubes leapt into it from a bowl. Gloria shook her head in slow disbelief. It was like a scene from a cartoon. Except it was real.

She watched as a fork bearing a sliver of bacon tiptoed up Lewis's arm and perched on his shoulder. Lewis turned his head and pulled the meat off the fork with his teeth. She noticed that in one hand he was holding a pipette. He placed its nose into a small dark object. Gloria squinted. It was a chocolate bar wrapper. The pipette filled with a blue liquid. Lewis squeezed the bulb at the end of the pipette and a single drop of the blue substance dripped on to a salt cellar. A shimmer of blue light passed over it. And suddenly it was alive! It waddled towards his plate and sprinkled salt on to the meal.

Lewis stood up. He said something out loud to the assembled objects. Gloria strained to hear. Had he said 'House heating'? 'House beating'? He walked to the door, which swung open of its own accord, and went through it, the living objects trooping after him.

House meeting, thought Gloria. That's what Lewis has said. He was calling a meeting of all his bizarre little housemates. In the instant before the kitchen lights went out, Gloria's eyes focused on the pile of *Chocky-Crocky* wrappers lying on the kitchen table. She paused for a moment, thinking, and then smiled before reaching into her pocket and drawing out a box of matches.

CHAPTER TWELVE
The Patient

It was the next day before they were allowed to visit Gabby's mum. The air inside the hospital was hot and dry. Gabby and Orville McIntyre sat on two plastic chairs in a waiting room. In front of them was a coffee table covered with old, torn magazines. In the corner was a children's play area. There was a clumpy jigsaw made of large wooden pieces, a small sad-looking plastic rocking horse and a toy telephone. Everything was battered, grubby, worn out.

A couple in their twenties sat opposite them, their faces dour and creased with concern. They held hands. Gabby tried not to imagine why they were there. Nurses and orderlies came and went, brisk and businesslike mostly, but occasionally sharing a private joke. Gabby looked at her watch for the fifth time in half an hour.

McIntyre closed his magazine and placed it back on the coffee table. He picked up another. 'D'you know,' he said, 'I actually think I rather like hospitals.'

'Why's that?' said Gabby without interest.

'Not sure really,' he said brightly. 'Something to do with the smell maybe. All starchy and official. Well ordered. Maybe it reminds me of public school.' He snorted with laughter.

Gabby let out a long sigh. After they had discovered the unconscious body of her mother in the park, McIntyre had, as an adult, assumed command of the situation and sent Barney home, claiming he would only get in the way. Gabby and McIntyre had ridden to the hospital in the ambulance with Gabby's mother. She was breathing, the paramedics had informed them, but not responsive.

A nurse in a crisp blue uniform approached them. 'Eleanor Grayling's family?'

'Well,' said McIntyre, 'I'm more of a friend than a—'

'I'm her daughter,' Gabby interrupted.

The nurse smiled. 'Come this way. You can see her now.'

With bitter and terrible irony, Gabby thought that the figure of her mother reclining in the hospital bed resembled a leaf. But it wasn't one of the glossy green leaves that Mrs Grayling used to decorate their home; it was pale and deathly, an end-of-autumn leaf, yellow-grey and so fragile you dared not touch it in case it crumbled to powder in your fingers. Her eyes were closed but not peacefully so – it was more as if they had frozen mid-blink, seized up. A plastic tube ran from her nose to an oxygen cylinder. Electrodes attached to her chest were connected to a small bank of machinery above which a flat computer screen showed flickering graphs and read-outs. Her breathing was faint and slow, each breath escaping in a tiny, distant-sounding sigh.

Gabby placed a hand on her own stomach. It felt as if there were a chunk of poisonous ice melting inside.

'It appears to be a form of coma,' said the nurse. 'Maybe some new reaction to her heart medicine, we're not sure yet.' She glanced at a clipboard hung over the end of the bed. 'You say you found her like this in the park?'

Gabby nodded. She sniffed and wiped her nose with the back of her hand.

'That's right,' said McIntyre brightly. 'Conked

out under a pile of leaves like a hibernating hedgehog, bless her.'

Gabby dug her fingernails into her palms. She found McIntyre's relentless cheerfulness misplaced and wearying. She wondered if he greeted every difficult situation with such infuriating good humour.

'Well, you can stay with her for a while if you want to.' The nurse gave Gabby a small smile. 'We're not sure if she can hear you, but it can't hurt to try talking to her. We'll give you a ring as soon as we know something.' She nodded to them and left.

Gabby reached out and felt her mother's forehead with the backs of her fingers. It was warm. That was good, she guessed. She had expected it to be cold. She pulled up a chair and sat beside the bed. 'I'm staying here,' she said to McIntyre. 'I'm not leaving her. I'm never leaving her.'

'Nonsense, Gabby,' said McIntyre. 'You can't. Be practical. You've got school tomorrow.'

'School?' said Gabby. 'Are you joking? School

doesn't matter at the best of times, never mind when my mum's in hospital. Forget school. I'll be fine here.'

'See sense, will you, girl?' said McIntyre and Gabby thought she could detect a note of irritation in his voice. She was childishly pleased to have provoked him. 'You heard the nurse: you can stay for a while, but there's no way you'd be allowed to stay here tonight. And nothing you could do if you did. And I should remind you that it's only my connections that are preventing you from being taken immediately into care.'

'I can sit with her,' said Gabby, her voice rising. 'I can hold her hand. I can talk to her. If she woke up and I wasn't here, she'd get all confused and upset. She'll want to look at some leaves. Can you bring some next time you come? I'd get them myself, but I have to stay here. Any kind of leaves will do.' Her eyes were glistening now, her voice trembling.

McIntyre laid a hand on her shoulder. 'We'll

bring her a lovely bouquet – but tomorrow evening, during visiting hours, and after you've been to school. You can see her every day, Gabby. No one's going to stop you doing that. But you'll have to go home and go to school in between. Eleanor would want you to carry on with life as normally as you can. You know I'm right when I say that, don't you?'

Gabby didn't meet his eye. She looked at her mother and then down at the floor.

McIntyre squeezed her shoulder. 'You're going to have to cope on your own, Gabby. Your mother needs you to be strong.'

Gabby nodded very slightly. She didn't feel like quarrelling with him any more. She half wanted to slip into a coma and escape from reality herself.

She looked up at the sound of footsteps. A tall, white-coated doctor entered the room. He was ridiculously handsome, with a rich tan and sparkling white teeth. He looked like he should be modelling pullovers in a catalogue rather than curing the sick. 'Hi, guys,' he said in a slick voice like a local radio DJ. 'How are we doing?'

'You tell me,' replied Gabby.

The doctor ran a finger along the monitor screen above Mrs Grayling's bed. 'Hmm,' he said. 'I'm afraid I can't give you guys great news. Although there's nothing really physically wrong that we can find, something – and we're not sure what – has happened to your mum's mind. It's shut down, a bit like a TV on standby. Not receiving.'

'So what can we do?' said Gabby.

'At the moment, nothing, I'm afraid,' said the doctor. 'But rest assured, guys, I shall let you know if there's any significant change in her condition. You know the way out, I take it?' He flashed his perfect teeth. Gabby wanted to punch them.

Barney rapped on the door with his knuckles. After a moment, it opened, revealing the strange world of swishing green leaves within.

'Hey, Vice-pres.'

'How are you coping?'

'Dunno if I am,' said Gabby. 'I'm just sort of existing. Everything's on hold. It's like nothing else matters while Mum's in hospital.'

'How is she? Did they let you see her?'

'McIntyre's just dropped me back from the hospital now; they finally let me in to see her, but he wouldn't let me stay long. The doctors don't seem to know what's wrong with her; she's just sort of existing, too.'

'Where's McIntyre now?'

'Gone.'

'You want to go for a walk?'

'Yeah. Hang on. I'll get my parka.'

The sun had slipped below the horizon, but the sky was still suffused with a pale-grey light. A sharp breeze tugged at Barney's hair and collar as if trying to attract his attention. They walked in silence. Barney was tempted to make small talk, but he sensed that Gabby was deep in thought and didn't want to interrupt her. They had walked barely two streets when they caught sight of a strange staggering figure in the distance. It waved at them frantically.

'Look,' said Barney.

'It's not, is it?' whispered Gabby. 'It is!' She ran up to the figure just in time to catch it as it collapsed. 'Hurry!' she shouted at Barney. 'It's Lewis!'

Gabby cradled the smaller boy's head as he lay on the pavement. His clothes, skin and hair were blackened with soot. He coughed with a deep rattling gurgle. She took her phone from her bag and tossed it at Barney. 'Call an ambulance.'

Barney caught the phone and began to fumble with it. 'How do you unlock the keypad?' he said. Gabby groaned. 'Give it here,' she said.

'No need, man,' said Lewis. His voice was thin and weak. 'I'm done for.'

'Don't be silly,' said Gabby. 'You're going to be fine. What happened? Have your mum or dad got a mobile? Do you know their numbers?'

'Mum left months ago,' croaked Lewis. 'Fed up with me, she said. Fed up with her life. Never knew my dad. I live on my own – well, used to ...' He coughed. 'There was a fire. In the garden. In the bin. Tried to put it out. Took ages. When I went inside, it was all gone.'

'What was?' said Gabby.

'That's why I was looking for you two,' said Lewis. 'I thought you could help me find it. Someone's pinched it, man.'

'Pinched what?' said Barney.

'The blue stuff,' said Lewis. 'The stuff that brings things to life.'

'Someone's taken it?' said Gabby.

Lewis nodded. 'I need it,' he said. 'Not just for

the things in my house. But for me. Y'see,' – he smiled weirdly – 'the blue stuff was in a lorry. It crashed and blew up and I think … I think I was hurt in the explosion. Quite badly burnt. But a tiny speck of the blue stuff landed on me. And now it keeps me going. Sort of repairs me. Stops the burns developing. Without it, I think I'd be in a whole heap of trouble.'

CHAPTER THIRTEEN
THE ASSEMBLY

The sun had been up for hours; Gloria had been up even longer.

She stood outside the school's main entrance and watched as the first few students arrived. Next to her on the step was a stack of freshly printed copies of the *Examiner*. The tops of her arms ached from her exertions. Her fingers were sore and blackened with ink.

Seeing her, the children exchanged wary glances, but Gloria smiled warmly and offered each a copy of the newspaper. 'Here,' she said. 'Special edition. No charge.'

'Really?' said one of the children, a feisty Year Nine girl with long red hair. She narrowed her eyes, as if expecting some trick.

'Of course,' said Gloria. 'There's no need to be so suspicious. Think of it as a gesture of goodwill to all our loyal readers. A little thank you for your support.'

'Oh,' said the girl. 'Right. Cool. Cheers.' She took the newspaper. 'Hey,' she said. 'It feels really cold!'

'The papers have been waiting here since the early hours of the morning when the printer delivered them,' explained Gloria. 'They may feel cold but believe me, they're actually hot off the press.'

The girl shrugged. She and her companions went inside.

Gloria allowed herself a small smile.

*

Barney was waiting for Gabby at the school gate when she arrived with Lewis.

'Morning, Vice-pres.'

'Hi,' said Barney. He nodded at Lewis. 'How are you?'

The small boy shrugged. 'All right, yeah. I think.'

'Did you find any of the blue liquid back at your house?'

'Just the teeniest little bit in the corner of an old *Chocky-Crocky* wrapper,' said Lewis. 'Everything in my house has stopped moving, man. Stuff needs a fresh dose of the blue liquid every week or it goes back to being just an ordinary object. I need it more often for some reason. Every day or so.'

'I even phoned Orville, told him we needed the Technoslime as a matter of life and death,' added Gabby. 'He said the government had got rid of the entire supply.'

'I thought you were going to take Lewis to the

hospital last night when you were visiting your mum?' said Barney. 'Couldn't they help?'

'I did,' said Gabby. 'They said there was nothing wrong with him.'

'But he's as cold as a block of ice!'

'They told him to put a jumper on.'

'Ah.'

'I got in touch with Ben, the photographer from the paper who we found hanging around outside Lewis's house, to see if he had any of the liquid. He swore he didn't take any. He sounded too scared to be lying. I don't know what else to do. Poor Lewis could conk out on us any second.'

Lewis shrugged. 'If it happens, man, it happens.'

'Someone at school might know something about the robbery,' said Barney.

'That's what I'm hoping,' said Gabby. 'Hey, is that the new *Examiner* you've got there? Maybe there's some clue in it. If anyone can spot a potential thief, it's Gloria.'

'Uh, yeah,' said Barney. 'She just gave it to me actually. I don't think you'll want to see it, to be honest.'

'Why not?'

Barney handed her the newspaper. 'I haven't read it all, but there's an article about you.'

Gabby stared at the front page. *10 Facts About Weirdo Greyling* ran the headline. There was a photograph of Gabby mid-blink with her eyes closed and her mouth hanging open. The article underneath read:

No, it's not a rare snap of a Yeti! This is, in fact, Gabrielle Greyling from Year Nine, without a doubt the biggest freak in the entire school. Here are ten fun facts we've found out about the kid nobody likes!

• Gabby was known as the Big Bossy Brainbox at her primary school. By her teachers!

- Gabby has the fashion sense of a colour-blind scarecrow!
- Gabby has zero (count 'em!) friends!
- Gabby would rather read books about something called 'quantum physics' than gossip about boys and pop music!
- Gabby has awful hair!
- Gabby holds meetings of a daft club she has created every lunchtime and in three years not a single person has joined! Talk about unpopular!
- Gabby can't name a single character in *Hollyoaks*!
- Gabby's mum is properly bonkers. No wonder her dad left them!
- Gabby once walked around school the whole day with a sign saying 'I am a massive idiot!' stuck on the back of her jumper and she didn't notice because she's so used to people laughing at her!

- Gabby will probably be a scientist or something stupid like that when she grows up instead of getting a normal job in a shop or as a cleaner or something.

Gabby groaned. 'Lovely pic. I look like a Neanderthal with indigestion. And they spelled my name wrong. But I don't really care what they say about me. I realise now. It's that stuff about Mum and Dad that makes my blood boil, though.'

'Is it true?' asked Barney. 'About you running club meetings every lunchtime for three years and no one ever turning up?'

She nodded. 'But they forgot you, didn't they? My one success.' She smiled and folded up the newspaper. 'Forget about this rubbish,' she said, dropping it into a nearby recycling bin. 'There are more important things to worry about. Let's start asking around about the robbery.'

The school bell rang.

Barney looked at his watch. 'Funny,' he said. 'It's ten minutes early.'

A familiar female voice rang out from the school's public address system. All the children in the yard stopped what they were doing to listen. 'There will be a special pre-registration assembly this morning,' it said. 'Go to the school hall immediately.' It repeated the message.

The hall was full to bursting with every child and member of staff in the school. The air was abuzz with rumour and speculation. Barney stood on tiptoe and tried to see above the crowd. Was the head teacher about to make some startling announcement? A small figure made her way through the jostling crowd and climbed the large wooden steps leading up to the stage. She cleared her throat loudly. The chatter began to die down and was replaced by a tense hush. 'Good morning,

191

everyone,' said Gloria. 'It's so nice to see you all here today.'

Gabby nudged Barney's arm. 'I don't know what this is about,' she whispered. 'But I don't like it one little bit.'

Suddenly, Lewis staggered backwards, stepping on to the toes of a Year Eight girl standing directly behind him. The girl called him a name and pushed him away. He dropped to his knees, a look of confusion on his face. 'I think I can feel the burns coming. It sort of itches '

'Let's get him out of here,' said Gabby. 'He needs some air.' She and Barney gripped Lewis by the elbows and guided him out of the hall and into the corridor. They sat him on the floor with his back to the wall. Gabby felt his forehead. 'He's still freezing cold. Is that good, do you think? Does that mean the blue liquid is still working?'

Barney shrugged. 'We have to call an

ambulance. He's obviously not well. Anyone can see that.'

Gabby cupped Lewis's chin and stared into his eyes, speaking slowly and clearly. 'Think, Lewis. Is there anywhere – absolutely anywhere – you can think of where you might have put any of the liquid?'

Lewis shrugged. 'It's all gone, isn't it?' His voice was weak. 'All the wrappers.'

The sound of singing came from inside the hall. Gabby peered into it through a window set into the hall's heavy double doors. 'She's making everyone sing! "All Things Bright and Beautiful."'

A loose thought jangled in Barney's mind. He frowned. 'What did you fill the wrappers up from?' he said to Lewis. 'What was the liquid in originally?'

'This big plastic tub thing,' said Lewis. 'That's what it was being kept in for transportation in the lorry. I brought it home from the field.'

'And that's gone, too?'

'That went days ago,' said Lewis. 'It was really weird, man. I hid the tub inside my mum's old grandfather clock and the next morning the whole clock had vanished.'

'The clock!' cried Gabby. She felt as if her heart had just been struck by lightning. 'I know where it is!'

'You do?' said Lewis. 'Cool beans.' He reached into his pocket and brought out a small brass key. He handed it to Gabby. 'The tub's inside the clock case. Hurry, man. Please.'

Inside the hall, the more musically gifted children and teachers were singing the hymn with gusto. Most of the rest were miming, wishing the wretched thing would end soon. A few of the more rebellious sixth-formers were quite openly not even miming, merely standing there with bored expressions and occasionally rolling their eyes to indicate how uncool they were finding it. Hymns were rarely sung at Blue Hills High. Someone had told the head teacher that the school's dusty Victorian hymn books were actually quite collectable items and he had immediately sold the lot on the Internet, using the money raised to buy a new sofa for the staffroom. This morning, the pupils and staff were singing from copies of the *Blue Hills High Examiner*. Gloria had made a last-minute copy alteration before the paper went to press and printed the words to the hymn on the back page.

Still feeling groggy, Lewis got to his feet and looked into the hall. 'All Things Bright and Beautiful' reached its conclusion and the last reverberations died away into silence.

On the stage, Gloria smiled her sweetest smile. She surveyed the rows of curious faces before her. 'What a lovely sight this is,' she said, 'to see everyone holding a copy of the *Examiner*. The entire school is here this morning, with the exception of the head teacher, Mr Siskin, who is temporarily indisposed. However, he gave his blessing for me to take this very special assembly. I have a simple message to communicate to you today. You see,' – her eyes glinted – 'I'm sick of you all.'

There were a few nervous laughs.

'No, it's true,' she went on. 'I've grown mightily sick and tired of the lack of discipline and respect for the rules in this school. Pupils chatter like magpies when they should be working; they run in the corridors; they sneak sweets to one another in lessons. In short, they *mess about*. And messing about is not to be tolerated.'

Now there were some indignant snorts. Near the back of the hall, someone made a sarcastic *ooooh* sound to indicate how unimpressed they were.

'SILENCE!' yelled Gloria at the top of her lungs. The sudden explosion of noise sounded like the detonation of a small bomb. Looks of terror crept across the faces of the younger children. 'That is precisely the sort of attitude I am talking about. Sheer contempt for common, everyday decency! I have tried in my humble way through my editorship of the *Examiner* to encourage an atmosphere of quiet humility in the school. I did this by bringing to wider attention the misdeeds of Blue Hills High pupils in the hope that a public shaming would convince them to see the error of their ways. But my best efforts have met with only partial success. The foolishness, the ill-discipline, the *messing about* goes on. But that all changes today. You see, I have found a new and exciting way of using the *Examiner* to improve school discipline. And from this moment on, messing about will become a thing of the past.' She clapped her hands.

There was a great rustling noise, like the beating wings of a huge flock of birds. The copies of the *Blue Hills High Examiner* that the staff and pupils were holding suddenly sprang into life, their pages flapping madly, and attached themselves to the faces of everyone in the hall. Many screamed but the sound was muffled as the newspapers wrapped themselves tightly round their heads like masks.

Out in the corridor, Lewis gaped. 'Crazy, man,' he whispered. A flapping copy of the *Examiner* skittered across the floor towards him like a small angry dog. He held out his arms instinctively to protect himself. The newspaper stopped at Lewis's shoe and Lewis had the bizarre notion that it was somehow *sniffing* him. Whatever the newspaper might have been looking for, it appeared not to find. It turned and skittered back up the corridor from whence it came. Lewis breathed a sigh of relief and peeped through the window into the hall once more.

People were clawing at the newspapers, trying desperately to rip them away. But the

black-and-white newsprint masks wriggled and writhed beneath their fingers, resisting all attempts at removal.

'Do not be alarmed,' Gloria was saying to her audience. 'I think you'll find that the more you struggle, the more uncomfortable you'll feel. Try to relax. Breathe. I don't want to suffocate anyone.'

A few people took her advice and ceased struggling. Small holes began to tear themselves in the newspaper clinging to their faces. They found they were able to breathe normally. Holes appeared over their eyes and they were able to see once more.

'That's it,' said Gloria. 'Perfect. Now,' – she looked at her watch – 'just time for you to troop back to your form for registration before the first lesson of the day. Don't worry, holes will appear in the masks at break and lunchtime to allow you a little refreshment. But only then. If you need to speak at any time – and I include teachers in this – your newspaper will automatically form a hole over your mouth so you can be heard. But, and I cannot stress this enough, only if what you have to say is deemed relevant to your education. You will not be allowed to speak simply for the purpose of idle chatter.'

'You're a lunatic!' cried a muffled voice. Lewis saw a tall boy – it sounded like that kid called Duncan who was always press-ganging younger children into playing his Honourable Deaths game – his head engulfed in newspaper, running towards the stage. 'You can't do this to us!'

'Watch, everyone,' said Gloria, 'and you'll see why I can.'

The newspaper around the boy's head tightened. The boy emitted a strangled wheeze. The audience gasped. The boy tried frantically to peel away the newspaper from his face, but it was no good. He sank to the floor, arms and legs flailing. Gloria watched impassively. His struggling subsided. Presently, he lay still.

Gloria clapped her hands. Holes appeared in the newspaper over the boy's face and mouth. He began to cough and splutter. 'Don't worry about him,' she said. 'He'll be hunky-dory. But please let this be a lesson. Rule breaking in any form will not be tolerated. At the end of school, the newspaper masks will remove themselves and hide in your schoolbags so that you may go home as normal. Do not try to alert anyone outside the school to this scheme or the newspapers will take drastic action. I hope I never have to spell out exactly what I mean by that. But I'm sure I can rely on your co-operation. Now off you go to registration.'

CHAPTER FOURTEEN
SCOLOPENDRA SUBSPINIPES

Racing along the quiet avenues of Blue Hills, Barney and Gabby skidded round a corner and collided with a tall, heavy-set man wearing dark clothing. He caught them both by the collars with his large strong hands. Barney noticed the radio, baton and handcuffs dangling from his belt.

'Good morning,' said the policeman. 'Would you two clowns kindly tell me what you're doing out of school?'

*

The pupils marched to their form rooms in neat lines, their footsteps the only sound in the long, echoing corridors.

Gloria headed for Mr Siskin's office and went inside without knocking. The head teacher was sitting immobile at his desk, a copy of the *Blue Hills High Examiner* clinging to his face. She clapped her hands. There was a ripping sound and a small tear appeared in the newspaper over Mr Siskin's mouth. 'Listen,' she said. 'Can you hear that?'

Mr Siskin's mouth twitched. 'Wha—what?' His voice was weak.

'Listen again,' said Gloria. 'I'll make it easier for you.' She kicked open the door to the office.

'I – I can't hear anything,' said Mr Siskin. 'What am I meant to be—'

Gloria interrupted. 'OK, I'll spell it out. What you are hearing is *no* running. What you are hearing is *no* shouting or screaming. What you are hearing is *no messing about*. What you are hearing is discipline. What you are hearing is education. The children at this school are going to learn today. They're going to pay attention. I guarantee it. How long have you been head teacher here?'

Mr Siskin paused, licking his dry lips. 'Please, Gloria, don't harm anyone. I implore you. There's no need for this foolishness. Really.'

'Answer the question, sir! How long have you been head teacher at this school?'

'About four years.'

'Four years,' repeated Gloria. 'Four years of your best efforts no doubt. Funny then how I, a mere child of twelve, can bring order to the chaos that is Blue Hills High in a single morning. Why were you unable to do that?'

'I did bring order,' Mr Siskin insisted.

Gloria snorted. 'You call what we had here order? It's only because of my work with the *Examiner* that this school could function at all!'

'Through blackmail and threats.'

Gloria flashed her sweet smile. 'All I ever did was tell the truth.' She glanced around the office, at Mr Siskin's expansive desk and at the rows of neatly framed certificates lining the walls. 'I like this office. I think I'm going to enjoy working here.'

'What?'

'It's clear that I should be the head teacher. I'm the only one who seems to understand the importance of adhering to school rules.' She glanced at her watch. 'Mr Pilbury's Year Ten history class is starting soon. He's teaching the decline of the Roman Empire. Why not pop along there, eh? You might learn what happens when leaders fail to maintain discipline.'

She clapped her hands and the hole over Mr Siskin's mouth sealed itself up. The newspaper covering his head clenched. Mr Siskin let out a muffled cry of pain.

'Room U11. Don't worry about not being able to

see. Just walk and the newspaper will guide you. Off you pop.'

Mr Siskin didn't get up. Instead, he clawed at the newspaper mask.

'I said, *off you pop!*' shouted Gloria. The newspaper clenched tighter and Mr Siskin went limp. Meekly he got to his feet and padded from the room, his shoulders sagging. Gloria closed the door behind him with the toe of her sandal.

As Mr Siskin made his way towards room U11, a pair of astonished eyes peered at him through a crack in the door of a supplies cupboard.

The policeman raised his eyes at them, expecting an answer. Gabby and Barney wriggled like landed fish. 'Well?'

'*Scolopendra subspinipes!*' cried Gabby without missing a beat.

'Excuse me?' said the policeman, frowning heavily.

'My friend here has *Scolopendra subspinipes*,' said Gabby, motioning to Barney.

Barney nodded quickly. 'It's true. I do.'

'And what might I ask is—?'

'It's a disease of the middle ear, of course,' said Gabby. She looked at the policeman as if he was a particularly foolish five-year-old. 'It's highly dangerous. Don't they teach you anything in police training college? He's left his medication at home and our head teacher has instructed me to accompany him while he collects it to make sure he's all right. Now can we go, please? We're in rather a hurry, if you don't mind.'

'How do I know you're telling the truth?' said the policeman.

'Here's how,' said Gabby. 'You keep us here wasting our time and when my friend keels over in agony, clutching his head and possibly suffering irreparable damage to his hearing, you can explain to his parents and his parents' lawyers and your chief officer exactly what you thought you were doing depriving an innocent schoolboy of his medicine! Would that satisfy you?'

The policeman considered this for a moment. He let go of their collars. 'Go on,' he said with a sigh. 'On your way.'

'Thank you!' said Gabby. 'A most sensible decision, officer. Thank you again and God bless!' She grabbed Barney's hand and pulled him away. They sprinted off down the avenue.

'Where did that ear disease thing come from?' asked Barney when they arrived at the railway bridge. He looked back the way they had come to make sure there was no sign of the policeman.

'First thing that came into my head. I just hope he never actually looks up *Scolopendra subspinipes* on the Internet.'

'Why? Is it not all that dangerous after all?'

'It's not even a disease. *Scolopendra subspinipes* is a kind of centipede native to Vietnam. My Uncle

Steve used to keep them. It was the only Latin name I could think of.' She grinned. 'Worked, though, didn't it?'

They eased aside the loose slat in the fence and climbed through.

The grandfather clock stood in the centre of the waste ground, its long wooden body glinting in the morning sun. Gabby noted wryly that it had moved another few metres since the last time she had seen it. She took the key Lewis had given her and slid it into the small metal lock halfway up its case. The door was stiff, but it squeaked open with a tug. The first thing she saw inside was the long pendulum swinging back and forth: the clock's ticking metal heart. And there, wedged at the back of the case, was a stout container made of transparent plastic. It was half full of a thick blue liquid. A crack in its front had been crudely repaired with adhesive tape. She reached in and took hold of the container. 'Barney, give me a hand with this.'

Barney held the bottom of the container and they lifted it out of the clock case and placed it on the ground. Gabby rummaged in the pocket of her parka. She drew out an empty *Chocky-Crocky* wrapper. 'I'll fill this and get it to Lewis right now. You find a good hiding place for the container and then come back to school and find me.'

'I would suggest secreting it in the bushes over yonder, where you placed your moving picture machine,' said a rich, ancient voice.

'Who said that?' said Gabby, looking around.

'I did,' said the grandfather clock.

Gabby gripped Barney's hand. 'Wow!' they said in unison.

'And may I say,' the clock went on, 'how grateful I am to you for removing that great weight from my insides. It was slowing me down terribly. I couldn't even speak with the effort of it all.'

'You're welcome,' said Gabby.

The grandfather clock peered down at her. 'Ah,

of course. It's you. I've seen you lurking around here before. I trust you are a little happier than when we first met, young lady?'

'I'm fine,' said Gabby. 'Look, I'd love to stop and pass the time of day with you, but the thing is our friend Lewis is dying and I need to get the blue liquid to him as quickly as possible'

'Lewis!' said the clock. 'That poor boy. Of course. Let's go.'

'What?'

'Climb on my back,' said the clock.

'You're having a laugh!'

'Not at all,' said the clock. 'Time is, I believe, of the essence – and after all who should know that better than a clock? Come! I'm quicker than I look, you know, especially now I don't have that container clogging up my innards.' The clock suddenly rocked on its small wooden feet and bent its great case towards Gabby, the wood flexing as impossibly as that of Barney's talking pencil. 'Climb aboard.'

Gabby looked at Barney. 'Do you think I should?'

Barney nodded. 'You're going to ride a clock! Of course you should do it!'

Gabby clambered on to the grandfather clock, her arms tight round the case under its face as if it was giving her a piggyback.

'Hold on,' the clock said. It rocked on its wooden feet a few times, as if testing Gabby's weight, and then waddled towards the fence with slow, heavy steps. 'Don't worry,' it told them. 'I do get faster than this.' Barney held aside the loose slat and the clock sidled through the gap with Gabby clinging on to its back like a baby monkey to its mother. There was a clanging chime and the clock began to strike a quarter to the hour. 'Time to go,' it said, and then with a sudden burst of frenetic speed, the grandfather clock raced up the avenue on its four wooden feet.

CHAPTER FIFTEEN
Time Flies

The grandfather clock hurtled along the streets of Blue Hills towards the school with Gabby clinging to its back. Never having ridden a clock before, she was somewhat unprepared for the experience. Its surface, like that of any object brought to life with Technoslime, was icy cold beneath her fingers and she found it best to protect her hands with the sleeves of her cardigan. Her knees banged painfully into the back of the case with every stride until she found a way to brace herself against a small wooden ridge near the clock's base. The wind streamed through her long curly hair.

The clock moved with rapid, bounding steps, its four small wooden feet clattering against the pavement. From within its case came the rattling of its metal pendulum and weights, a steady clank like the pounding of a mechanical heartbeat.

They rounded a corner – the clock improbably pirouetting on a single foot – and passed the policeman they had encountered earlier. Gabby couldn't resist. 'Morning!' she called cheerfully.

The policeman stared, open-mouthed. He felt his knees give way a little. Had he been in a film, he thought, then at this point he would probably have fainted, his eyes rolling upwards as he slid gracelessly to the floor. But this wasn't a film. It was reality. And a teenage girl really had just ridden past him on a grandfather clock. He watched as the improbable timepiece careered to the end of the road and vanished from view behind a row

of parked cars. He imagined the response he would get if he radioed into the station and reported what he had just witnessed. No, the policeman decided, there was only one possible strategy for coping with this, he was absolutely sure – and that was to pretend it had never happened. He steadied himself, took a deep breath and resumed walking the beat, his eyes alert for anything unusual.

In the staffroom, the few teachers who were not taking classes sat in silence, their newspaper masks tight around their faces. One or two were marking piles of exercise books, tiny holes in their masks allowing them to see.

Gloria looked on with quiet satisfaction and stirred her tea. She was drinking out of Mr Siskin's mug. On its side in large chunky letters it said *World's Greatest Head Teacher*. She figured he didn't need it any more.

There was a clattering noise out in the playground. She went to the window and peered through. What she saw made her chuckle.

Gabby entered through the school's main door and headed up the corridor towards the hall. There was no one about. 'Lewis?' she called. 'Are you there?'

The reverberations of her voice were the only answer. There was something odd about the school this morning. Some strange absence of atmosphere. A shiver ran down her spine.

To quash the notion, she paused at the first classroom she came to and peered in through the window. Children sat in rows at their desks, quietly copying down information from the black-board while a teacher drew a diagram of a Roman hypocaust. Their faces were encased in news-paper. They moved with mechanical sluggishness, zombie-like.

Gabby's jaw flopped open.

'*Pssssst.*'

The sudden noise made her jump. She spun round. No one. 'Hello?'

'Pssssst! Gabby!'

The sound seemed to be coming from inside a large walk-in supplies cupboard. She pushed the door open with a cautious finger. A hand shot out and pulled her inside.

'Lewis!'

'Ssshh! Keep it down, man. She'll hear you.'

'Are you OK? I brought the liquid.' She handed Lewis the *Chocky-Crocky* bar wrapper. He speedily unfurled one end and let a single viscous blue drop fall out on to the palm of his hand. A blue shimmer passed through his entire body.

'I am now, man,' he said with a smile. 'Have you seen what's going on here?'

'I saw a classroom filled with people with newspapers stuck to their faces.'

'It's Gloria,' said Lewis. 'She's made the *Examiner* come to life. It's controlling everybody. It must have been her who stole the liquid!'

'What? That's insane!'

'The newspapers stick to you. But they can't see me somehow. Maybe because I'm already infected with the blue stuff. She's taken over the school.'

'But she can't do that!'

'She has, man. Every single pupil and teacher has one of those newspapers on them.'

'Then we've got to stop her, Lewis! We *have* to stop her.'

'I really wouldn't bother if I were you,' said a pleasant voice from outside the cupboard. 'It would only be your own time you're wasting.' The door opened, revealing Gloria standing outside with her mug of tea. In her other hand she held a copy of the *Examiner*. Two teachers with newspaper-clad faces were standing beside her. They took hold of Gabby and Lewis's shoulders, dragging them out of the cupboard. 'Come on now. Off to your lessons.'

'What on earth have you done?' cried Gabby, struggling against the teacher's grip. 'You stole Lewis's liquid! He could die without it!'

Gloria shrugged. 'I'm sorry about that. But not much. It would be a very small price to pay for bringing order to the school. And it's not as if he's going to be missed. Children like Grimy Grome never are.'

'You're a monster, Gloria,' said Gabby. 'You're inhuman.'

'And you, Gabrielle Grayling, are an irritant. Have you seen this week's *Examiner*? You're front-page news, you know. When I was writing it, I thought it might finally knock a little sense into you, but I see now I shouldn't have bothered. Mere public humiliation couldn't deter someone who's so used to it already. Fortunately, I have a new method of dealing with unruly pupils.' She threw the newspaper to the floor and clapped her hands. There was a rustling noise and it sprang to life, its pages flicking and twitching. 'Why don't you read all about it?'

The newspaper slithered along the floor towards Gabby. Gabby strained against the grip of the teacher, but could not free herself. Then she heard a chime. She felt a breeze on her face as something whistled through the air and slammed onto the newspaper, flattening it. There was a clank of mechanical innards, a flash of brown wood. Gabby gasped.

The grandfather clock loomed over Gloria. Beneath its four wooden feet the newspaper squirmed, trapped. 'Playtime's over,' said the clock in its rich voice. 'I suggest you release the two children now.'

Gabby's heart sang. 'You heard the clock! Let us go, Gloria.'

Gloria's face showed not the slightest trace of

anxiety. She smiled her sweet smile. 'I don't think so,' she said and threw the hot tea from her mug over the grandfather clock. The clock froze instantly as the hot tea splashed into its wooden face and dripped down its front. It stood there immobile and silent, a mere piece of furniture once more. 'I should have done this when I had the chance,' said Gloria and gave the grandfather clock a shove.

'Don't!' cried Gabby.

The clock toppled over backwards, falling like a great tree, and hit the floor of the corridor with a jangling, shattering crash of wood and metal.

Gloria chuckled. She winked at Gabby. 'Now go to your lesson.' She clapped her hands.

The newspaper slithered up Gabby's leg and folded itself around her face.

CHAPTER SIXTEEN
SOUNDS LIKE A PLAN

Barney crouched behind a car on the scrubby patch of grass and peered over its bonnet. When he had arrived at the school two minutes earlier, he'd seen a teacher and a group of pupils with weird white masks marching like zombies across the playground from one building to another. Such a bizarre sight might ordinarily have made him laugh, but something in the slow, blind stomping of the children sent an arctic shiver down his spine. It was oddly pathetic and defeated. This wasn't some weird drama studies exercise, or even a game, Barney could tell. Something very strange was going on.

A tiny sliver of painted wood emerged from a crack in the school's main entrance doors and hopped rapidly across the yard towards him. It rolled under the car and emerged at the other side.

'So did you manage to get inside? What's happening?'

'It is most strange,' said the pencil. 'It appears all pupils and teachers have newspapers stuck to their faces which are severely limiting their ability to speak and move.'

'Newspapers?'

'Indeed. I should imagine the newspapers are made sentient by the same substance that animates me. A young girl appears to be in control. She has taken over the head teacher's office.'

Barney's eyes narrowed. 'A young girl? What did she look like?'

'Shoulder-length blonde hair, blue eyes, a white Alice band, dimpled cheeks, pointed chin ...'

'Gloria! It must have been her who stole the blue liquid,' said Barney. 'That was a very good description, by the way.'

'I'm a pencil. I am good at details,' said the pencil looking very pleased with itself.

'Any sign of Gabby and Lewis?'

The pencil nodded, its tip waggling impossibly. 'Gabby is in her class and has one of those newspaper masks attached to her. Lewis does not and has been banished to the head teacher's office. He appears to be in good health.'

'So how are we going to get in there and free them without being spotted?'

'I have no idea,' said the pencil. 'While I am grateful to you for animating me, please bear in mind that this is my first espionage mission. Forgive me if it does not come naturally.'

Barney felt the *Chocky-Crocky* wrapper in his

coat pocket. He had filled it from the plastic container in case of emergencies. 'Hot water seems to cancel out the effect of the blue stuff. Where could we get enough hot water to douse the entire school?'

'I hope that was a rhetorical question,' said the pencil, 'because I haven't the foggiest.'

Barney rubbed his chin. 'The caretaker's little room is right at the back of the school near the canteen. The door's on the outside so we won't have to go into the school and risk being seen to reach it. There might be a hosepipe there. If we connect it up to a hot tap in the toilets, we could be in business. We could even bring it to life and get it to squirt all the masks itself. What do you think?'

'That, sir,' said the pencil, 'sounds like a plan.'

'Crop rotation prevents a decrease in soil fertility, as growing the same crop repeatedly in the same place eventually depletes the soil of nutrients. A crop that leaches the soil of one sort of nutrient is followed during the next growing season by a dissimilar crop that returns that nutrient to the soil or draws a different ratio of nutrients, for example, rices followed by cottons.' The teacher's voice was flat, muffled, as he read.

Through the two small holes in her newspaper mask, Gabby looked up from her textbook at the diagram chalked on the blackboard. As she did so, a yellow-white flash from the window dazzled her. She turned her head and saw the sun emerging from behind a spray of white cloud, shafts of gold connecting sky and earth like pillars of light. Its beauty sang to her. A distant idea at the back of her mind began slowly to resolve itself. There was something she was meant to be doing. She was supposed to be helping someone, wasn't she? Who? She knew and she knew that she knew – but the relevant information had been tidied away into a far corner of her brain, just out of reach.

'Don't look at that,' cooed the newspaper into her ear in a sickly whisper, breaking her chain of thought. 'That's irrelevant to your education.' The holes in the mask began to contract. The world darkened and she suddenly began to feel light-headed. 'Why not look at the blackboard or your textbook, *mmm*?' She turned her head back to look at the blackboard and immediately the eyeholes in the mask expanded, letting in air. She filled her lungs gratefully. 'Good girl,' said the mask. 'This is your favourite lesson, isn't it?'

'It's my favourite lesson,' repeated Gabby, suddenly feeling much better. She kept her voice down so as not to disturb the rest of the class.

Barney rattled the door handle of the caretaker's room. He grunted in irritation. 'Locked!' He looked around the empty schoolyard for something he might use as a crowbar.

'If I might make a suggestion?' said a quiet voice. It was the pencil. Barney had stuck it behind his ear.

'Go ahead.'

'The blue liquid may be of use.'

'I don't get you.'

'The door, sir. It may prove amenable to persuasion.'

'Of course! You're a genius!'

'I am merely an HB, sir. Jack of all trades.'

Barney took out the *Chocky-Crocky* wrapper and loosened the adhesive tape holding it closed. He squeezed out a single drop of blue liquid and let it drip on to the door handle. The liquid seeped quickly into the metal and a shiver of blue light passed over the door.

'Yes?' said the door, sounding rather gruff.

'Can you open, please? We need to find a hosepipe.'

'No,' said the door firmly.

'Aw, what?' said Barney. 'This is an emergency! I need you to open right now. Come on.'

'I have an important job to do, you know, mate,' said the door. 'There's a lot of valuable tools and equipment in here. I have to protect it. I can't go opening at the drop of a hat for the first person who comes along. It would be more than my job's worth.'

'But you have to do what I say. Aren't I your parent?' asked Barney. 'Didn't you – you know – *imprint* on me?'

'What if I did?' said the door indignantly. 'Still got a mind of my own and a job to do, haven't I? As part of the school, I have a duty to it.'

'I haven't got time to stand here and argue with a stroppy door!' hissed Barney. He jerked the handle angrily. It was stiff. He noticed that the door's hinges were rusty and coated in cobwebs. An idea occurred to him. 'I could oil you, you know.'

'What?' said the door uncertainly. 'What did you say?'

'I said I could oil you. Look at the state of your hinges. Bet they must be nearly seized up, judging by all that rust. And I can barely turn your handle. When was the last time the caretaker oiled you?'

'Well,' said the door. 'Now that you come to mention it ...'

'Let me guess – never?'

The door mused. 'You're right, mate,' it said. 'In all the years I've guarded the caretaker's gear, he's never stopped to think that I might need some attention. He's always too busy swanning off fixing radiators and broken windows to think about me.'

'That's a terrible, terrible pity. Look, I just need to grab a hosepipe from inside. It won't take more than a minute of your time. If you open up and let me get it, I'll splash a drop of oil on to those creaky old metal joints of yours. What do you say?'

In response, there came a *clunk* as the door unlocked itself.

'Thanks very much,' said Barney. He opened the door and went inside. He flicked on the light. The room was tiny, little bigger than a cupboard, and filled with broken furniture and cartons of paper towels. The air smelled musty. In one corner lay an ancient lawnmower encrusted with mud and grass. The walls were lined with wooden shelves. On them Barney saw tins of creosote, a bottle of methylated spirit, an old toolbox – and a dusty green hosepipe. 'Fantastic!' he cried, taking the hose down and checking it. It seemed in good condition.

The door swung shut and locked itself.

'Hey,' said Barney. 'What are you playing at? Let me out!'

'I've been thinking about this a bit more,' said the door, 'and I'm not entirely comfortable with the idea of you just walking off with the caretaker's hosepipe. I mean, what if you just ran away with it? Where would we be then? I think it's better if I keep you here until the caretaker comes back and you can ask him personally.'

'What?'

'It's not that I'm accusing you of theft or anything. It's just, well, you can't be too careful, can you?'

'But I need to go NOW!' hissed Barney, trying not to raise his voice. 'The whole school has been taken over by an insane twelve-year-old girl and a lot of slithering newspapers! I'm going to set everyone free.'

'I wouldn't know about any of that,' said the door. 'I'm just doing my job. Speak to the caretaker when he comes back.'

'When's he coming back?'

'Any day now, I expect. A week, tops. I understand he's gone on holiday to the Isle of Skye.'

'WHAT?' Barney rattled the door handle furiously. 'You can't keep me trapped in here that long! I'll starve to death!'

'Maybe you should have thought of that before you took it upon yourself to pinch other people's hoses.'

'I only need to borrow it for a little while!'

'*Tra la la*,' sang the door. 'I can't hear you.'

Barney slammed his hand against the door. 'This is not funny. Open up right now.'

'Oh, shush,' said the door. 'I'm getting tired of your prattling.'

Barney sighed and slumped against the wall.

'This is indeed a most obstinate door,' said the pencil.

Barney looked around for something with which he might conceivably pick the door's lock, but drew a blank. Then he noticed the mouldering old lawnmower in the corner. He took hold of its chunky handle, feeling the machine's weight and force. He gave a push and its metal blades rotated with a loud clacking sound, drumming against the bare concrete floor and sending up tiny blue sparks.

'What are you doing?' asked the door nervously.

WHUMP! Barney slammed the lawnmower into the bottom of the door. The wood creaked under the impact. Flakes of paint fell away.

'Hey now!' cried the door. 'Stop that!'

'Not until you let me out,' replied Barney. *WHUMP!* He rammed the lawnmower into the door again. More sparks flew from the machine's innards.

'Never!' said the door. 'This mindless violence isn't going to make me change my mind, you young thug!'

'Oh, no?' said Barney. 'We'll see about that.' *WHUMP!* He thrust the lawnmower at the door with all his strength. The whole room vibrated and the items on the wooden shelves rattled. As he was pulling back the lawnmower to make a fourth lunge, the bottle of methylated spirit toppled from its shelf and fell, shattering, on to the lawnmower's sparking blades. There was a hiss and the lawnmower's innards erupted in flame. Barney felt a flash of intense heat singe his eyebrows and hair. He staggered back in speechless panic, hitting his head on a shelf. Some of the flaming methylated spirit had splashed on to the cartons of paper towels and these now burst into hissing, crackling flame. Smoke began to fill the tiny room.

Barney hammered on the door. 'You've got to open up! Right now!'

'You'd like that, wouldn't you, hosepipe thief?' said the door sniffily. 'No. I don't think so, sonny. You're going nowhere.'

CHAPTER SEVENTEEN
A Rainy Day at Blue Hills High

Barney searched desperately for anything in the tiny room he might use to douse or smother the flames. Already the heat was almost unbearable and the thick black smoke was making it difficult to see.

'If I might offer a suggestion, sir?' said the pencil calmly into his ear.

'Feel free to chip in at any time,' said Barney through clenched teeth. He pulled his jumper up over his nose to shield himself from the smoke.

'This may be another occasion when the blue liquid proves useful.'

'On what?' said Barney. 'What am I going to bring to life? The fire?'

'Yes.'

'*What?* Would that work?'

'How could we possibly know until we try?'

'Good point.' Without further hesitation, Barney took out the *Chocky-Crocky* wrapper and opened its adhesive tape seal. He flicked the wrapper at the fire, sending several drops of the blue liquid flying at the pale, oily flames. The flames hissed and turned a striking blue colour. The air was instantly full of high chattering voices.

'Hello!' said one of the voices.

'Hello!' said another.

'Hello there!' said a third.

For a moment, Barney forgot his fear and simply laughed with delight. *The flames were talking to him!*

'So,' said the first flame. 'Is there anything in particular you might want us to heat up?'

The harsh electronic note of the fire alarm rang out across the school. Gabby and the rest of her history class sat calmly at their desks and continued with their work, ignoring it. Their teacher, Miss Fairchild, got up from her desk, intending to lead the class safely and without fuss to the fire assembly point in the schoolyard. Instantly, the holes in the newspaper mask over her eyes began to shrink. 'Don't worry about the alarm,' cooed the newspaper in her ear. 'I'm sure Gloria will issue instructions over the PA system soon enough. Please return to your seat and continue with the lesson.' Obediently, Miss Fairchild sat down again.

Sure enough, a few moments later, Gloria's voice barked from the large PA speaker mounted above the classroom door. She spoke with a distinct note of irritation. 'All staff and pupils must make their way outside to their normal fire assembly points. This is not a fire drill. All staff and pupils, outside, please. *Now*. Let's not waste any more time than we absolutely have to.'

'You heard her,' said Miss Fairchild to the class, raising her voice to be heard above the alarm. 'Form an orderly line.'

As one, the children got to their feet and tramped towards the classroom door. There was a sudden hiss and jets of water began to rain down on them from the ceiling. The water was piping hot.

'Ignore it,' said Miss Fairchild. 'It's just the automatic sprinkler system. Hurry up now and we can be outside before we get too ...' Her voice trailed away into silence. She and her class stopped in their tracks, seemingly paralysed by the jets of water.

Gabby felt strangely woozy. She clapped a hand to her head. The newspaper mask was soaked with water. She pulled at it. Her fingers went straight through the soggy paper. She took hold of it in both hands and ripped. It came away from her face easily, breaking apart in her hands. She blinked, dropping the sodden lumps to the floor, and wiped her eyes. The water rained down on her from the sprinkler nozzle, as hot and invigorating as a bathroom shower. She lifted her face to it and let it wash away the last traces of newspaper.

'How are we doing?' cried one of the flames.

'Brilliantly!' said Barney. Five minutes earlier he had persuaded the door to the caretaker's room to finally unlock itself and release him. This had not been due to any sudden improvement in Barney's argumentative skills, but because he now commanded a small army of sentient flames, who would have quite easily burnt out the wood surrounding the door's lock had it not complied.

The flames were now dancing along a thin metal pipe that ran along the exterior wall of the

school's main building. This was the pipe that fed the emergency sprinkler system. All over the school, freshly heated water was pouring from the sprinkler nozzles. And all over the school, children and teachers were clawing the strange wet newspaper masks from their faces and wondering just what on earth had been going on that morning. They stood around in groups, dazed, the hot water raining down on them and soaking their clothes and books. Slowly coming to their senses, their teachers hurriedly directed the pupils to go outside and assemble in the yard. They trooped out and lined up, chattering in nervous whispers and wringing out their sopping jumpers. Soon, every class in the school was outside.

'That's enough,' said Barney to the flames. 'You can stop heating the pipes. It's worked.'

The pale blue flames hopped from the pipes and landed on the faded tarmac of the yard, melting it a little. 'What would you like us to heat up now?' one of them asked in its cheery high-pitched voice. 'Or burn,' said another. 'We're also good at burning things.'

'Erm, nothing really,' said Barney. 'You've done an excellent job for me today, but I don't need anything else from you. Is that OK?'

'No problem!' said the flames in unison. There was *ffffft* sound and they vanished, leaving only the faintest wisp of oily blue smoke hanging in the air. Barney grinned. A hand tapped him on the shoulder.

'Hey, Vice-pres.'

'Gabby!' Barney threw his arms round her and then quickly let her go when he realised how wet her clothes were.

She laughed. 'My head feels like it's full of porridge. Or papier mâché. What just went on? Something odd has happened – hasn't it? – and I've got a feeling it's something to do with you.'

'Don't you remember?' said Barney. 'The

newspapers came alive. You'd brought the blue stuff back to help ... *oh, no!*'

'What?'

'Lewis! I made the sprinklers drench everything in hot water to cancel out the effect of the blue stuff. But that's the stuff holding his injuries at bay! Come on!'

They raced to the head teacher's office. They found Mr Siskin kneeling beside the unconscious figure of Lewis, desperately pummelling the boy's chest with the flats of his hands. There were lurid red-black burn marks on Lewis's face. 'Breathe, boy!' he was yelling. 'Breathe, Grome!' He saw the two children standing in the doorway. Gabby's lip started to tremble. She took hold of Barney's hand. 'I've phoned for an ambulance,' Mr Sisken said gravely. 'But I must warn you to expect the worst. I can't seem to find any pulse.'

'Let me see,' said Gabby. She knelt down beside

Lewis, feeling his forehead with her fingers. She looked up at Barney and mouthed the word 'distraction'.

Barney nodded. 'Oh, my good golly!' he yelled. 'Look, Mr Siskin! How did this grandfather clock end up here?'

'Grandfather clock?' said Mr Siskin. 'Really? Where?' He went to the door.

'Just here in the corridor. Look. It's all broken.'

'Oh, yes. Extraordinary!'

Quickly, Gabby took the *Chocky-Crocky* wrapper and squeezed a drop of liquid from it on to Lewis's forehead. A wave of blue energy rippled through his body. The burns on his face vanished instantly. He sat up with a start. 'Hi,' he said. 'Is that a *Chocky-Crocky* bar? I'm starving!' He reached for it eagerly.

''Fraid not, mate,' said Gabby with smile. 'This one's empty.'

'Good lord!' cried Mr Siskin. 'It's a miracle!

Grome, my boy! How good to have you back in the land of the living!'

Lewis shrugged. 'Have I been away?'

Barney held out his hand for Gabby to high-five him, but she missed his hand at the last second and swung her own back to clap herself on the forehead. 'Where's Gloria?' she said. 'She's got her own supply of the liquid. She could still be up to all sorts of mischief with it.'

They scoured the corridors without success, their feet pounding on the wooden floor. A flash of blue light through a window caught Gabby's eye. She touched Barney's arm and pointed. He started to laugh.

Outside in a corner of the playground, hidden from the assembled classes still shivering in their wet clothes, was a ring of blue flames on the tarmac. The flames burned tall, forming an eerie cylinder of fire. Trapped within, Barney and Gabby could see a small frightened figure. There was a look of fierce indignation in her large blue eyes. They went outside to get a better look. 'Howdy!' said one of the flames brightly. 'We were on our way out when we caught her trying to escape. We thought you'd probably want to have a word with her.'

Before Barney could reply a voice barked loudly from somewhere just outside his field of view. 'Down on the floor!' it yelled. 'All of you. Now!' Three men came round the corner. Two were soldiers dressed in combat gear and carrying rifles, the third a civilian. The soldiers stared in amazement at Gloria's flame-prison for a second but then, as if snapping out of a daze, they advanced on Barney and Gabby, pushing them roughly to the ground with the palms of their hands. As he went down, knees and elbows banging on the tarmac, Barney realised that he recognised the civilian.

It was Orville McIntyre.

CHAPTER EIGHTEEN
A Cheap Trick

Barney and Gabby sat on two simple wooden chairs. Across a scuffed wooden table from them sat McIntyre, his chin cupped thoughtfully in his hand as he listened to their story. They were in an interview room at the local police station. McIntyre had had no trouble in commandeering it for his purposes, a single flick of his MOD identity card producing simpering awe from the local constabulary. The soldiers had searched the two children, confiscating their *Chocky-Crocky* wrappers.

Gabby and Barney finished their story. McIntyre leant back and lit up his pipe. 'No doubt,' he said, 'you are worried about your friend Lewis.'

'He'll be fine,' said Gabby. 'As long as he gets a constant supply of the blue liquid. You can supply that, can't you?'

McIntyre shook his head. 'All remaining quantities of Technoslime have been incinerated. Including the batch from the crashed lorry that you hid in the trees near Lewis's house. I have no discretion in this matter.'

'But the Technoslime stops his injuries from forming!' said Gabby. 'He needs it! Are you saying there's nothing we can do?'

McIntyre smiled a small knowing smile. 'He'll be fine. Fascinating child, that Grome boy. Did you know he actually imprinted on the sky?'

'What?' said Gabby. 'What do you mean?'

'Our chaps found this out from talking to him. He was lying on his back in a field when the

Technoslime first touched him and brought him back to life. He opened his eyes and the first thing he saw was the sky above him. On some level, he actually believes he *is* the sky! Explains why he talks like a refugee from a sixties hippy commune.'

'But how will he survive without the blue liquid?'

'We've been working on that,' said McIntyre. 'Thing is, when the blue stuff brings a simple object to life, the effect usually lasts a week or so. It's what Technoslime was made to do. When it brings something as complex as a human being to life, however, it requires a great deal more calculating power, and so the Technoslime gets used up quicker. That's why he needed the stuff so often. But not any more, thankfully.' He reached into his pocket and drew out a small metal tin. It looked like a container for mints. He opened its hinged lid, revealing a mass of tiny orange capsules. Gabby and Barney raised their eyebrows.

'This is new. A highly concentrated form of Technoslime,' said McIntyre. 'Roughly eighty thousand times stronger than the blue liquid. Its effects are more or less permanent. We've given one to Lewis. He's going to be all right.'

'What about Gloria?' said Barney. 'What happens to her?'

McIntyre snorted. 'The girl's a genius. Unbelievable IQ. But a psychopath along with it, sadly. No conception of the feelings of others. She's going to remain locked up for some considerable time while we – er – *study* her.'

'And how do her parents feel about that?' asked Gabby. 'You just taking away their daughter?'

'Extremely grateful!' said McIntyre and guffawed loudly. 'No, really! You should have seen their faces. It was like they'd won the lottery!' He guffawed again. 'Anyway, how are you two now after today's events? No ill-effects, I trust?'

Barney gave Gabby a look that she couldn't fathom. 'Something strange has happened to me,' he said.

'Oh yes?' said McIntyre.

'I can fly.'

'What? Are you serious, boy?'

'Really?' said Gabby. 'You never mentioned this before! It's quite an extraordinary claim. Are you able to provide extraordinary proof?'

'Watch me.' He stood up and went to the corner of the room. He took a moment to compose himself and then, in a single graceful movement, his feet lifted a few centimetres off the floor.

'Good lord!' exclaimed McIntyre as Barney floated gently back to the floor. He got up out of his seat and put a hand to Barney's forehead. 'You're normal temperature. No Technoslime animating you. Do it again.'

'Sure.' Once more, he rose into the air, his

feet dangling impossibly. He hung suspended in nothingness for a few seconds and then touched down again.

'Astounding!' said McIntyre. 'How do you do this? Imagine if we could perfect this power for the army! No one could stop them!'

'That's not going to happen,' said Barney.

'Oh?' said McIntyre in a less than friendly way. 'And what makes you think that, laddie? We're very good at extracting information from people.'

'Because it's a cheap trick,' said Barney. 'A simple conjuror's technique. It's called Balducci levitation. Look it up.'

'So you were just wasting my time?'

Barney grinned. 'Yes. Good, though, wasn't it?'

McIntyre let out a groan. 'Go on. Get out. The pair of you. Your head teacher's cancelled school for the day. Go and pay your mother a visit, Gabby.'

He led them out.

When they were safely away from the police

station, Gabby burst into laughter and enveloped Barney in a crushing hug. 'You are a genius, Barney Watkins. You really are.'

Barney smiled, his face flushing red. 'Possibly. So how many of the orange capsules did you swipe while his back was turned?'

Gabby held out her hand and showed him.

The air inside the hospital was hot and dry. The only sounds were the muted chatter of the staff, the patients and their visitors, and the occasional beep of a heart monitor. Then there came a sound that no one had heard before. Several people stopped their conversations and turned their heads to listen to it. It was a high, fluting sound. But a very small one, too. A tiny warbling arpeggio of tinkling silvery notes, beautiful as birdsong. It drifted across the arid ward like a crystal stream suddenly erupting from desert rock.

Deep within Eleanor Grayling's mind, clouds of pain and confusion began to disperse like morning mist in sunlight. She became aware that she was lying in a bed, her head propped against large soft pillows. The sound, the glorious sound, was calling her, calling her back. She opened her sleep-heavy eyes as far as she was able – which was not far. But it was far enough to see the singing leaf standing on her bedpost, and behind it, the beaming, tear-streaked face of her daughter.

A few days later, Barney, Gabby and Lewis sat eating a picnic after school on one of the low, grassy hills that overlooked the town. The early evening sun was warm and golden, sliding down the sky like a sliver of butter over a hot crumpet.

'How are things at home, Lewis?' asked Gabby, unwrapping a chocolate bar.

'Real cool, baby,' said Lewis. 'All the gear in the house is totally looking after me. The stove apologises for shooting that coal at you, by the way. It says it was just trying to protect me.'

'No worries,' said Gabby. 'It's about time I replaced this old parka anyway.'

Barney was busy drawing a sketch of the view, or rather, he was looking on attentively while his pencil drew the view itself. 'Is that a pleasing likeness, sir?' it asked.

'It's great,' said Barney. 'Love the use of perspective. I've a feeling I'm going to get good grades in art this year.'

'No doubt, sir.'

The paper plane swooped down and perched on Lewis's shoulder, pecking occasionally at the image of the eagle on Lewis's tie, the image on which it had imprinted in the back of the crashed lorry when Lewis first brought it to life.

Gabby reached into her bag and took out the latest copy of the *Blue Hills High Examiner*. The front page bore a picture of her and Barney and the headline *Grayling and Watkins Save School From Maniacal Plot*. 'I still can't believe it,' she muttered.

'What?' said Barney.

'They actually spelt my name right.'

There was a sudden chiming sound. The three children looked up to find the grandfather clock waddling up the hill on its four wooden feet. It had been freshly repaired and lacquered, courtesy of Orville McIntyre, and its ancient wood gleamed like new.

'We mustn't be staying out too late, Master Grome,' it said. 'There's homework to be done, I'll be bound, eh?'

'Gimme a break, man,' groaned Lewis. He flopped back on to the grass and stared at the sky. 'Can't you just savour the view for one minute?'

The grandfather clock stopped and took in its surroundings. 'Yes, I suppose it is rather a splendid view, is it not? You can see my mother from here.'

Gabby frowned. 'Its mother?'

'The church,' said Lewis. 'That's what it could see through the window of my house when it came alive. It thinks the church is its mother. That's where it was going across the waste ground when you found it.'

Gabby clicked her fingers. 'Of course! Ha!'

Barney looked at his watch. 'Speaking of mothers, we'd best be off. You know how they worry if you're out too long.' He scooped up the pencil and slid it into the inside pocket of his coat. He and Gabby said their goodbyes to Lewis and his odd new guardian and set off down the hill.

'The town looks so peaceful from up here,' said Gabby. 'So normal.'

'It *is* normal,' said Barney, 'if you don't count the events of the last few days. Otherwise, it's as dull as anywhere else.'

Gabby shook her head. 'You think so? Check

this out.' She pulled out a handful of papers from her bag. There were random scraps of A4, pages torn from exercise books, printouts of emails, even scribbled-on bus tickets. She handed them to Barney.

'What's this?'

'Impossibilities.'

'What?'

'Strange stuff that people reckon is happening in Blue Hills. Since the Gloria business, they just walk up to me in school and give me the details. It's mad – ghosts, aliens and a lot of even crazier stuff. They want me to look into it for them.'

Barney looked through the sheets of paper. 'These can't all be true.'

'No,' said Gabby with a grin. 'But we won't know for sure until we investigate them.'

ABOUT THE AUTHOR

Mark Griffiths grew up in North Wales. At age 17 he sold his first comedy material to Radio 4. At 18 he was writing for *Smith & Jones* on BBC 1. He co-created and co-wrote BBC Radio Wales's political sitcom *The Basement* with Cai Ross. He's written two stage plays – *The Lullaby Witch* and *The Impossibility Club* – as well as one for BBC Radio 4 – *Leona Cash*, and was one of the writers on Charlie Brooker's TV series and book *TV Go Home*. He studied philosophy at the University of Reading. His interests include magpies, English muffins, the pop group Cardiacs, weasels, dinosaurs, limes, theatre, coelacanths and seeing the moon during the day.

LOVED GEEK INC.?

THEN READ ON FOR A SNEAK-PEEK OF MARK GRIFFITHS'S MAD-CAP SPACE ADVENTURE...

Somewhere deep in outer space . . .

Bolts of pure energy rained down on the tiny starship, splintering and twisting its fragile hull wherever they touched it.

The huge black battle cruiser *Gharial* lingered a moment, toying with the smaller craft, and then unleashed another furious burst of fire. Arcs of blue-hot light scythed towards the tiny ship from *Gharial's* guns, blasting three of the smaller ship's four engines into scrap and sending molten fragments spinning off in all directions.

The last remaining engine tried to drag the little starship to safety, but a further blast from its attacker sliced it clean off the ship. The detached engine coughed out a thin wisp of vapour and expired. The little craft sat paralysed against the harsh blackness of space.

One more hit would obliterate it.

Aboard the *Gharial*, a radio spat out a burst of static.

'We are receiving a message from the stricken vessel, O Marvellous Fanged Dictator,' warbled Captain Yellowscale, bowing so low that his lizard nose scraped the shiny metal floor of the command bridge.

From high upon his throne made of enemies' skulls, Admiral Skink, Grand Ruler of the Swerdlixian Lizard Swarm and commanding officer of the *Gharial*, surveyed his underling with huge, cold eyes. 'I suppose they want to plead for their wretched lives,' he said with a snort.

'You are indeed correct, O Wisest and Most Violent Lizard Emperor,' said Yellowscale. 'Shall I relay the message?'

'Why not?' said Admiral Skink, popping

a Dysonian sparkworm – his favourite snack – into his huge jaws. 'I could do with a chuckle.' He bit down on the sparkworm, sending its delicious flammable juices oozing down his throat.

'It shall be done, O Gorgeous and Powerful Vanquisher of the Ganthorian Battle Mammoths,' cooed Yellowscale and stabbed a button on his control panel. A thin, desperate voice echoed around the bridge.

'We have no hostile intent,' it said. 'Repeat – we are not hostile. This is a scientific vessel from the planet Squipdip. We are here merely to study the formation of comets in the Poppledock Gas Cloud. We are nice people with families and pets. We recycle. You have nothing to gain from our destruction.'

Admiral Skink roared with laughter. 'Open

a communication channel to this ship,' he ordered. 'This is going to be fun.'

'Channel open, O Wondrous Reptile Monarch,' said Yellowscale.

'Now hear me, Squipdipians,' said Admiral Skink. 'Your kind really makes me sick. Prancing about the universe collecting your weedy scientific data. Studying gas clouds? What use is that to anyone? Why aren't you out there disintegrating stuff and waging war like any self-respecting civilisation ought to be doing, eh?'

There was a pause. The radio crackled back into life. 'We do not believe in violence,' came the reply from the Squipdipian ship. 'We believe in peaceful co-existence and the gathering of knowledge. We have learned much from our research inside the gas cloud, information that may be of great benefit to your species. Let us go free and we will share it with you.'

'Pah!' spat Admiral Skink. 'I've heard some feeble bluffs in my time but that must surely be the most pathetic and transparent of all! Captain Yellowscale – blast that ship into extremely small pieces. Collect the bones of the dead. I wish to make them into a coffee table to go with this throne.'

'Begging the humblest of all possible pardons, O Victorious Sultan of Pain,' said Yellowscale, picking at the stitching of his imperial war-jerkin, 'but our spies have reported odd goings-on in the Poppledock Gas Cloud of late. I venture gently to suggest that we listen to what this Squipdipian scum has to say – at least before we mash them to bits. It could be to our advantage.'

'So, just to clarify the situation,' said

Admiral Skink, 'I, Admiral Skink, the Most Powerful and Deadly Warlord in All Creation, gave a direct order to destroy the Squipdipian ship and you, a worthless underling unfit to scrape the space-barnacles off a second-hand moon bus, are questioning that order. Is that the gist of it?'

'O Mighty Iguana-Faced Doombringer,' stammered Yellowscale. 'No offence was meant by—'

'Yes or no?' said Admiral Skink.

Captain Yellowscale sighed. 'Yes,' he said and winced.

'Come here,' said Admiral Skink, motioning to the area in front of his throne with his huge clawed hand. 'Stand before me.'

'At once, O Magnificent Terror of the Skies,' said Yellowscale as he scuttled to where his master was pointing.

'Do you know what the penalty is for insubordination aboard this starship?' asked Admiral Skink.

'Alas, O Supreme Lizard Warrior,' began Yellowscale. 'I do not.'

Admiral Skink opened his mighty jaws and unleashed a gigantic torrent of fire. The very air itself frazzled and singed. Where Captain Yellowscale had stood a split second earlier there was now only a small heap of smoking ashes.

'I hope that answers your question,' said Admiral Skink and popped another Dysonian sparkworm into his mouth. They were extra-hot ones – just the way he liked them. 'Now hear me,' he bellowed at the Squipdipian ship. 'I am a warlord. What I do not conquer, I destroy. You have nothing worth conquering. That leaves me only one option.'

'Please! You do not have to do this!' said the voice from the radio.

'I'm afraid,' said Admiral Skink, 'that if I am to maintain my reputation as the most unspeakably evil tyrant ever to draw breath in this vast universe of ours, you'll find I do.'

He jabbed a button on the arm of his throne. The Squipdipian vessel exploded in a dazzling flash of light.